Ten Stories of
Mystery – Suspense
Adventure – Intrigue

Ten Stories of Mystery – Suspense Adventure – Intrigue

An Eagle Falcon Publication

By
Dalward J DeBruzzi

E-BookTime, LLC
Montgomery, Alabama

Ten Stories of Mystery
Suspense – Adventure – Intrigue

Copyright © 2016 by Dalward J DeBruzzi

All rights reserved. No part of this book may be reproduced or transmitted in any form or by any means, electronic or mechanical, including photo-copying, recording, or by any information storage and retrieval system, without permission in writing from the copyright owner.

This is a work of fiction. Names, characters, places and incidents either are the product of the author's imagination or are used fictitiously, and any resemblance to any actual persons, living or dead, events, or locales is entirely coincidental.

Library of Congress Control Number: 2016908592

ISBN: 978-1-60862-652-6

First Edition
Published September 2016
E-BookTime, LLC
6598 Pumpkin Road
Montgomery, AL 36108
www.e-booktime.com

Contents

The End of the Rainbow 7

The Unlucky Draw 20

Fatal Beauty 43

Grasping For a Fortune 86

Identity of a Coward 113

The Improvident 120

Cryptic Suicide 137

The Sabbatical 203

Perspicacity 218

The Substitute 227

The End of the Rainbow

Teddy Trimble was a self reliant young man, steady in matters of industry, gainful employment, but unsteady in his tendency to take liberties in ignoring moral conventions. He took advantage of everyone he could; people inferior in intelligence, vulnerable in strength, resources, or low social standing, unfortunate souls with low self esteem. He avoided anyone who even hinted at an eleemosynary tendency. Teddy was in his early twenties.

On a shiny warm, spring day a little before noon Teddy was insouciantly strolling toward Eberharts Drug Store. Walking along to the drug store as he drew near he was passing a three story building that housed a lady's millinery store on the ground level, exhibiting a varied array of attractive hats, some with plumage, some beaded, a few feathered, a display to tempt style cognizant females. On the second floor a neon sign hung in front of the windows that announced, "Quick Cash." The third floor had curtains, drapes and blinds in the kitchen window identifying it as an apartment.

As his eyes traveled casually up and down the building for a final look his eye caught a sad looking little girl sitting off to the side on the cement stairs leading down to the basement apartment. Her forlorn, unkempt, shabby, dirty appearance touched him, even though such a feeling for him was an aberration it was not deeply felt, it was only a mild emotion. Considering his past, the flickering of compassion was a phenomenal reaction for him, totally uncharacteristic of him. He never gave money to mendicants on the street, never bought moochers in taverns a drink, never contributed to charities like the Red Cross or UNICEF, he was only a contributor to his own bank account and retirement fund. In Teddy Trimble's thinking, he was number one, and no one else was of consequence. His complex list of perverted priorities was the result of a sparse childhood and a family structure that favored his brother and sisters, not deliberate, but he was a casualty of timing, inattention, favoritism, lack of encouragement, less than equal and considerate treatment resulting in a miserly obdurate point of view and an absence of a tender heart for the needy and the deprived and unresponsive to needy children. After all, he bore the pain and he survived didn't he? Mutual love was an unknown stranger to him, the joy of sharing and giving unknown to him. He became fairly successful despite the unfair and emotionless early years of his childhood, and his feeling was that others could achieve success by great effort like he did. The fleeting pang of pity he felt looking at the soiled, neglected little girl aroused a shred of mild curiosity. "Do you live around here little girl?"

Sitting with her hand under her chin, looking down at the ground, she pointed with a finger of her free hand towards the door of the basement apartment.

With an unaccustomed inquiry into someone else's obvious distress, Teddy, after noticing the thin child's pale look, gauntness, spiritless, hopeless, despairing looking countenance proffered the question to find out what he wanted to know, "Did you have a nice breakfast this morning?"

Ten Stories of Mystery – Suspense – Adventure – Intrigue

The waif's upper lip raised a bit and a tear trickled down her face, making a rivulet through the grime on her face. Teddy was shocked at the obvious neglect this confirmed. Teddy had received his answer. With unaccustomed compassion in a soft patronizing tone he asked, "Do you have family?"

When no answer came, Teddy somehow felt a predicament, an exigency not to be ignored which was a feeling strange for him. He reached down, taking the thin little hand and leading her the five steps down from street level to the door of the basement apartment. Holding the softly sniffling little waif by the hand he knocked with his free hand. Not getting a response, he leaned down to the little girl and asked, "Is there anyone home?"

The despairing little girl, without looking up, spoke for the first time, "Only mommy."

Teddy still wrestled with mixed feelings about the tentativeness of his decision to venture into something like this, but the dispute in his mind was tilted to be adventurous with a motivation of a willing tinge of altruism. Teddy, in the unfamiliar territory of the good Samaritan, was momentarily undecided how to proceed. Looking at the needy little conundrum down at his side, he boldly knocked again, much sharper and longer than before. Having daringly decided his next course of action if there was no response, he turned the door knob and led the little girl into the darkened basement apartment. He flipped the light switch to on. No light came on, but he heard a faint rustle in the next room. A young girl not much out of her teens advanced to the doorway and stood there with a sickly, pale face wobbly and tottering. When she swayed weakly reaching out for support, she began losing her balance. Teddy caught her and gently laid her on the rumpled bed that was against the far wall. The child ran to her mother and buried her face into her bosom, crying and embracing her.

Teddy looked around the room quickly thinking about what he should do with an unconscious young woman and a little sobbing girl. In desperation he took the young woman's hand, not sure of what else to do, but began rubbing it to increase circulation, thinking it may help revive her. He didn't know what else to try. He observed her features as he massaged her hand, while desperately reassuring the little girl, "Now, now, she'll be fine, don't worry."

Teddy's attention was alerted as he observed the heart shaped face, the long eyelashes, the little, pertly, thin, finely shaped nose slightly upturned in fashionable style, her soft brown hair curling around her curved, graceful throat. Teddy with a jolt realized he was interacting with a human being of whose presence subconsciously increased his zeal and appetite for continuing his altruism which made his efforts quite compensatory considering that he concluded this was quite something that he got himself involved in.

The ashen faced young woman still lay motionless and the tiny girl continued sobbing. Teddy went to the kitchen sink. While dampening a towel he looked at the bare cupboards, noticed the stove wouldn't light with the gas valve turned off. He slowly felt the increasing gravity of two vulnerable souls mired in deep distress. There was no cooking gas, the electricity was turned off, and he noticed the absence of any cooking and meals having been prepared. Stunned at the evidence of the humbling, shameful scarcity of their existence, Teddy carried the dampened towel, sat alongside of the bed, gently dabbing it to the young women's forehead. The cold compress caused the young woman to stir. Her long eyelashes fluttered a few times into the darkened room, she opened her two hazel brown eyes, and putting an arm around her little girl she murmured, "My sweet Tessie." Her eyes shifted over, looking at the vague outline of Teddy Trimble as her eyes focused gradually, she said, "Fainted didn't I?" She continued feebly, in a barely audible voice, "It could happen to anyone," she whispered, "who has not eaten much in three or four days. Try it and you'll see what I mean."

"Yes, you're right of course," Teddy said, synchronously patting her arm in agreement. He smiled at little Tessie. "Don't go outside little one." Addressing the weary young woman he said, "Don't get up, I'll be right back." He hurried out the door, leaped up the stairs two at a time, with a feeling that felt strange to him, but good.

He soon came back with huge bags of groceries from the delicatessen and the super market. He kicked at the door. Little Tessie opened it and let him in. He brought hot chicken soup in cartons, milk, bread, cocoa, tea, an order of ribs, cold cuts, canned goods and some fresh fruits. "It isn't sensible to go without food for three or four days," he gently counseled. "You have a little girl to think of." She eagerly picked up a rib. "No, no," Teddy said in mild admonition, "you're not ready to handle that yet." He poured out some steaming chicken soup in her bowl and little Tessie's bowl, poured each of them a glass of milk. He said, "You must start with something easy after four days of going without much or you'll get sick." He smiled and said, "If you're real good you can have a rib tomorrow. If you don't mind, I'll join you for dinner I'm hungry too."

Eating with the young mother and her daughter who were indeed eating food that he provided them with gave Teddy sensations of satisfaction that, while incomprehensible to him, nevertheless released emotions of a nature that were never before experienced by him.

The girl and little Tessie ate with good manners considering their famished state, but their eyes blazed with the passions of animals that had made late kills and wanted to catch up. Teddy was for some reason relaxed in this strange situation. His normal reaction of detesting giving alms or charity was supplanted by vestiges of concern, with a hitherto unused attitude of helpfulness. Strange to him as this was it was even stranger that the woman seemed to react as if Teddy's help and his presence was normal which both pleased him but caused traces of anxiety. The mere hint of someone expecting dependence on him disturbed him. The uncomfortable emotion passed, then normal conventions of human behavior began to assert itself and the girl began telling Teddy her woeful story. Her name was Lillian Ballard, married at sixteen, after five hectic unhappy years little Tessie's father ran off. Her hours at work were cut short due to poor business, her inability to pay all her bills, eat properly and take care of little Tessie properly, resulted in irregular and excessive absenteeism and lost wages, resulting finally in losing her position.

"Wow," Teddy said compassionately, "I think you're lucky to be alive after going through all that."

The girl took on a pained look. "It was very painful," she said.

"How about your parents, brothers, sisters, relatives?"

She shook her head. "None, except for an uncle in Florida whom I haven't heard from in twenty years, I have no one. I'm all alone."

Teddy nodded. "I know the feeling. I am too."

She smiled unexpectedly with a commiserating look. "Please forgive me for saying this, but I feel glad you are for some reason."

This offering of noting a compatible condition they both were in was pleasing to Teddy. A compatibility was established that gave rise to all sorts of speculations in Teddy's thoughts which he cautioned himself could cause him embarrassment if his instincts and judgment proved inaccurate. Teddy felt a feeling of pleasantness thinking that this was a thrust from the girl for a common item between them. He liked the sensation.

"Mommy, I'm sleepy," little Tessie said. Teddy lifted her up and gently laid her on the bed with her head on the pillow and drew a blanket over her. He felt the gaunt girl shouldn't lift the child in her physical state. He wondered where all these charitable and considerate feelings were coming from. They were new to him.

She looked at Teddy with gratitude, then said, "I'm very tired and sleepy too, but I am feeling better."

Teddy didn't want to leave because his emotions had been aroused, but he said, "Well then, I'll be going. Get a lot of rest, it will help restore you."

He extended his hand and she enclosed his hand with both of hers. "You know Tessie and I can never thank you enough."

He detected the searching, the wishing, the pleading in her eyes that supplanted words. While her pleas were wordless he said in a congenial tone, "Lillian, I guess I'd better check on you and Tessie tomorrow to be sure you're alright."

Her face brightened. "Oh that's comforting to hear. Are you sure you want to?"

Teddy couldn't think of how to say exactly or how to fashion the words to explain his feelings, without saying things that would sour the prospects of the situation so he said nothing. He just looked into Lillian's expectant eyes, smiled a slow

Ten Stories of Mystery – Suspense – Adventure – Intrigue

warm, sincere smile, while nodding slightly a few times.

When Teddy paused at the door ready to leave, she said, "What made you bring Tessie in and take an interest in us? Do you usually do these kinds of surprising things?"

He reflected on her question for a moment and shuddered. He flinched, he would not like this woman to know what his usual reactions were in a situation like this, but he also thought, what if someone else had stumbled on Tessie and they would have fallen into other hands? The thought disturbed him. Not knowing what to say exactly, he merely said, "No, I never have really. Ordinarily I wouldn't have. I don't really know, Lillian, it just happened, one thing led to another, then I met you, and from observing the circumstances I guess just responded to it. If I wouldn't have I never would have discovered or realized that it's not just ourselves that consist of our existence and our comfort in it, but the answer and interaction with others is part of the answer. Very frankly, I feel Lillian as if you and Tessie are the ones who've helped me more than I helped you." They exchanged warm expectant smiles, each thinking happily of tomorrow, then Teddy went out the door with a luminous expression on his face.

Teddy's elation was partially the new identification of satisfaction that can emerge from interacting with someone you enjoy, the thoughts of the prospect of getting to know them better, to spend time with them to continue the pleasure that he felt when with that person encouraged his interest. What amazed Teddy was the expenditures he knew would occur deterred him not in the least. Teddy, in the flush of his sanctifying good fortune was totally unaware that he was one of the anointed, gifted ones who found his pot of gold.

The Unlucky Draw

The world in 1848 was turbulent and changing. The revolt in Paris, France forced the abdication of Louis Phillipe, revolution in Vienna, Metternich resigns, the Communist Manifesto is issued by Marx and Engels, first settlers arrive in New Zealand, serfdom abolished in Austria, United States under the Treaty of Guadalupe Hidalgo acquires California, Utah, Nevada, Arizona, Colorado and Texas from Mexico for a large indemnity.

The two compadres had partnered now for three years. Among other things they punched cows together on a small ranch in Texas near the Rio Grande in Del Rio Texas for a man named Nate Embry from Ohio who was running small herds up north to Abilene, Kansas. On their last drive Colt Florian and his partner sold the herd in Amarillo, Texas and kept going with the money. They robbed the stage on the run between Sweetwater,

Texas and Elk City, Oklahoma. They also hunted buffalo and scouted for General Crook. Both partners had a common aversion to settlements, towns or anywhere people were. They prided themselves on their rugged constitutions and sturdy resistance to the harsh weather in winter and the sweltering hot summer years, never living indoors.

Circumstances sometimes can accumulate and foil the health of even the most sturdy and healthy man as it happened to Colt Florian in March of 1867. While the partners were hunting buffalo, three days of unseasonable cold, freezing sleet and snow engulfed them in their camp catching them without an opportunity to construct a more permanent dwelling, even as they were thinking the unusual cold snap would end, seeing it was almost April, but it didn't. Colt started coughing the first day and late that night his throat became scratchy. He started coughing up clumps of green phlegm the following morning. His partner kept the fire up with a buffalo chip fire, but later that night Colt became delirious, drifting in an out of consciousness, looking weaker and weaker.

Early the next morning the sky had cleared and pale sunshine helped abort the unseasonably cold snap and a rapid warm up began, but Colt shivered and shook, kept coughing up clumps of green phlegm and continued body wracking coughs that left him weak, delirious, with an ashen, whiteness to his sweat covered face, hinting of death. The partner watched as Colt tried to rise on one elbow, then fell back down, babbling and mumbling incoherently, drifting in and out of consciousness, with his forehead covered with beads of sweat, looking white, ashen and the look of a dying man. His partner leaned down. "You need a doctor."

Colt whispered, "No, I'll be fine, I'll be fine," and lapsed back into sleep again. The partner had been thinking for some time now and when he heard the Ovaro and the dappled mare stamping with an occasional snort he made a decision. He loaded the fire up with additional buffalo chips, put another buffalo robe around his partner, saddled up and rode off seeking the nearest town.

Several hours later a Conestoga wagon with a man, his wife, a young girl and boy came creaking and bumping along over the rise, spotting Colt's fire. "Hello in the camp," shouted Ben Harken.

"Call 'em again," Mary Harken said.

"Hello, can we come in?"

No answer.

"Why Ben, that man ain't moved, he looks ill to me." She got down from the wagon, knelt down, and put her hand on Colt's forehead. "Why this man is close to heaven, Ben."

"Is he dead Ma?" said little Tommy Harken.

Mary ignored the question, turned to her eleven year old daughter Emily, "Fetch three blankets from the wagon, honey. Hurry."

Mrs. Harken wrapped Colt with additional blankets and for the first time he was warm enough to accumulate body heat for healing. She then put several handkerchiefs over Colt's nose to filter the cold air providing additional opportunity for his body to retain necessary heat for healing. All that night he perspired heavily, drifted in and out of lucidity, making babbling sounds.

When the thin blue line of light appeared across the horizon the next morning Mary Harken, Ben's plump wife, had a large cauldron of soup steaming on the blazing

Ten Stories of Mystery – Suspense – Adventure – Intrigue

fire with the rabbit and the prairie chicken that Ben shot the previous evening. She had put some wild onions and mushrooms in. Every time Colt looked awake she spoon fed Colt a few spoons of piping hot soup from a bowl that Emily held for her. She had to use two hands to hold his head up.

He was still hurting from an aching throat, sore lungs from the wracking, constant coughing, but on the fifth day was talking and sitting up. His first thoughts were of his partner's treachery, leaving him to die. He never once thought his faithful friend and partner Swift Elk would steal their money and abandon him. A terrible feeling of vengeance flooded over him thinking what he would do to Swift Elk for his betrayal.

The Harken family was from Avon on Bristol in England, members of the English Anglican Church. Striking Colt's camp was a mistake. They were off their intended course by about fifty miles too far south. Mary Harken laughed, "Mr. Florian, I always say the Lord moves in mysterious ways. There was a reason why he put us off course, why it was to help you." Then she laughed warmly and agreeably.

"Well I don't know about that," Colt laughed, "but I do know you folks sure saved my hide. I was all done if you wouldn't a come along."

"It was God's hand, not ours," Ben Harken said with a sincere, believing, sanctified countenance as he looked up slightly towards the sky with a look of total dedication in his faith and mission.

The next day the Harkens, Ben, Mary, Emily and Tommy, all gathered around Colt while Ben Harken gave benediction for Colt's recovery. Colt knew it was for his benefit, but he didn't know how to participate so he just stood with his head down trying not to reveal his sanctimonious feelings. He kept his hands clasped in what he thought was a religious stance while Ben delivered the thanks to the Lord. The goodbyes were brief and the Harkens left, creaking over the rise and out of sight, leaving Colt pondering what his next move was.

When he checked his saddle bags, he saw with amazement the full amount of money he and his partner had robbed from the stage with the money from selling Nate Emry's herd. He was puzzled why he didn't take it, knowing he lit out and left him to die. Well, leaving him to die was reason enough for vengeance when he caught up to him, but leaving the money raised a number of questions in his mind. Several unanswered questions now raced through Colts head. Why would Swift Elk not take the money? Where did he go?

Colt was feeling a bit stronger now, the wind had shifted to the south, helping to erase the unseasonably cold winter snap. The sky was an ocean blue, the sun shining, but the nice weather did nothing to pacify and ease the pain of the treachery of his partner leaving him to die. The pain of that ran so deep it increased his thirst for vengeance. He was saddened when he thought about how he and his partner met. He had found him tied to a tree in the northern part of the llano Estacado. He had been beaten, tortured, was near death for one steer in his possession that he found on the open prairie crippled, thinking he was more in need of the meat than the wolves. When he cut him down, nursed him back to health, they partnered awhile then took an oath of sworn friendship for life. So much for sworn friendship and loyalty, he thought.

Colt was only 24 years old, still shaky from a slight fever, even swayed in the saddle as he plodded toward the nearest settlement. He had his father's blond Swedish hair, his mother's pleasant friendly Irish face, and looked older than he was due to his weathered face, large size and mature behavior. He had already killed eleven people, nine white men, one Indian and one Mexican. One man was a card sharp in Laredo who was a nephew of the sheriff. Though everyone said it was a fair fight, Colt had to shoot the sheriff to stay off the gallows. A month later when the ram rod of Nate Embry's found him in the northern llano Estacado in a small cantina, he tried to bring Colt back to Del Rio, Texas for charges and Colt killed him. The others died in the robberies he and his partner committed. The Indian tried to steal his horse and the Mexican turned on him cause he stole his girl.

Colt never could understand how he got into the messes he got into. It seemed like he had little or nothing to do with it, it just developed without any help from him, but it happened. Colt conveniently projected all causes of his troubles to others. In his mind

Ten Stories of Mystery – Suspense – Adventure – Intrigue

he was just an innocent victim. As he cantered along, he adjusted his low brimmed flat black hat after he wiped off the heavy perspiration, which was still plaguing him from his lingering mild fever. He was dressed overly warm for the mild day, but felt comfortable, wanting to rid himself of the fever completely. He had on wool pants, wool shirt buttoned up to the neck, a scarf around his neck, low heeled boots that he preferred which gave him more stability than high heeled boots.

As he neared Lakin, Kansas, a town on the Arkansas River, he didn't think too much of it at all. There was only one street, a few low roofed houses, four commercial buildings, a copse of trees on both sides of the town, a few trails leading away from town in different directions. It was after dusk and a few lights were showing in windows, towards the end of the one street the faint sound of music came from the large clap board building on the right. Even though the town looked poorly, they were advanced enough to have a lively dance hall with bar girls that were also whores where a man could have a good time. There were only seven horses tied in front. A light night, but understandable because it was a Tuesday night. Weekends were much livelier. It sounded inviting, but he had no intention of stopping. He touched one his sharp Texas rowels to his dappled mare and she pushed forward.

Glancing to his left in the darkening sky a thin ray of light from a nearby cabin showed something up high, slowly turning, being nudged by the soft breeze. He reined his dappled mare slightly to the left and approached. He wondered what the hanged man did to deserve such a gruesome end. As he neared and his eyes adjusted to the dark, he was shocked at what he saw. He said, "Oh, oh, Christ no, no." The corpse was his partner, the half breed, Swift Elk. Things were a little clearer now, but there were still many answers he needed to fill in to get the whole story. He didn't know what Swift Elk did to deserve this, but he had to find out the reasons. He had to know why he was hung. He owed his partner at least that, even if he finds out he had abandoned him and was heading out, which he pretty much dismissed that thought from his mind.

He tied his horse in front of the shabby looking saloon called the "Oasis," and strolled in the open door. There were only two customers inside. The interior was dank, gloomy, with a crude bar of rough lumber. Wearing an apron once white, now soiled with stains all over it, was a large, fat, round shouldered, bald man with a large nose with veins visible all over it, chewing on a cedar toothpick leaning on the bar with his elbows looking at Colt with a leery suspicious look reserved for strangers in a small town watching him sit down without a greeting. Colt with a slight nod, sat down, ordered chili, beans and beer. When finished he lit a cheroot and sat back, trying to look comfortable. He was hoping the reticent bar keep would have opened with some questions, but he didn't so Colt, needing information, led off. Even though he was still groggy he kept his hand steady as he lifted his beer to his lips, then putting his glass down, said, "Real nice little town you have here."

"Humph, glad you think so. Nobody else does."

Colt responded, "Why those cattle pens outside of town makes it look to me others think this town is something."

"Well, we thought so too, but last year and the year before we had Indian raids, lost some folks around here too, the Kansas City bankers and the cattle shippers left us quicker than a steer in quicksand. Mister, them pens were never used once, then the government rerouted the rail spur and we were left high and dry and all because of them damn Injuns."

Colt leaned back in his chair, blew a stream of smoke up, "I ain't never heard of a railroad shifting course because of an Indian raid or two. It could have been any number of other reasons."

"Mebbeso, but we folks here in Lakin think it wuz Injuns. Why, the barber pulled out June of last year, a week later the printer closed up the newspaper, then the dang dentist left. The whole damn town's dying. Why if it wasn't for the dance hall and the whores bringing in some business this whole town would blow away." He looked closely at Colt, "You sound like a Southerner. You a Reb?"

Knowing this was Union country, Colt said, "Maryland. I was with 135th Maryland under Beauregard." This lie satisfied the fat man. Trying to sound mildly curious, Colt drawled slowly, "Oh, by the way, I saw a man strung up on my way in here. What happened?"

"That was no man, that was a stinkin' injun who got what he deserved." The fat man stroked his chin, laughing. "Why, the dumb blanket head walked into the dance hall bold as a white man demanding a doctor. He was told several times to leave, but he refused, kept mumbling about the doctor. Well sir, Big Ed LaTour and Elias Connelly got some of the patrons together and whetted their appetites for a hanging and did that stinkin' injun proper and put him away right and proper."

"Hmmm, Big Ed LaTour and Elias Connelly. I suppose leading citizens here, huh?"

"Oh yes. Big Ed owns the harness shop and Elias owns the mercantile and the Bar 20 Ranch. They're two of our leading citizens. They support our local businesses, there at the dance hall almost every night and in here almost every day too."

"That so. Didn't you have a sheriff here that could have taken a hand and stopped it?"

"Yes. That would be Heney Grimes, but he wouldn't interfere. You see his sister-in-law was killed in the last Cheyenne raid."

"I understand."

"Well, what you don't understand is nobody around here wanted to stop it. Why, the reason for that is in the raids around here we had women raped, tortured, abused, maimed, disfigured and killed. Why would anyone want to stop it?"

Colt looked at the man, knowing pointing out that all Indians were not killers would be a waste of time so instead he smiled while secretly thinking how much he would enjoy shooting him. Without a comment he walked over to the bar, put a bill down in front of the fat man, and got satisfaction in the fact he was paying him with stolen money. "Thanks for the grub. I'll be movin' along now."

"Cowboy?"

"Done some."

"Buffalo hunter?"

"Done some."

He strolled out and swung aboard the dapple mare. He looked in the direction of his partner. "Old partner, I'm sorry I ever doubted you." He understood now what he should have realized before, that when Swift Elk left and didn't take their loot he was going for help. Well, his partner deserved better than getting murdered just for trying to help him.

Colt knew from all the campfires he shared with Swift Elk that although he proved many times he was fearless, brave and loyal, his friend Swift Elk had one horrendous fear of being improperly presented to the Great Manitou which would condemn his spirit to wandering forever. Colt meant to see that his friend was presented properly.

The anger in Colt was so intense he forgot all about his receding fever, trotted over to the lonely hanging corpse, scrambled up to a branch above the one that Swift Elk was hanging from, threw a rope over it, tied it around under the arms of his compadre, cut the other rope and lowered him gently to the ground. Carrying Swift Elk a few miles out of town, Colt fashioned a funeral pyre, piled branches on all sides of it, and under it. He stood looking at his good friend and partner lying on top of the bier wrapped in a blanket, lit the mound and sat and watched it blossom up in a huge orange, smoky flame. He sat patiently watching the fire progress, burn brighter and brighter as it caught on, remembering his friend's never faltering loyalty all the while they were together. A few hours later while the last embers were smoking and going out leaving only ashes with tendrils of smoke curling up, he vowed then and there to exact a terrible vengeance on the people who murdered his companion.

He went to his horse, took a Navy Colt 44 model out of his saddle bag, laid it on the ground with his Remington 44. He was partial to both for their proven accuracy and balance. He cleaned and oiled each weapon carefully, checked their action several times, inserted cartridges in each cylinder, strapped on his Remington 44, put the Navy Colt in his belt and swung aboard the dappled mare. He headed back to town. It was dark, near midnight, the piano was plinking away, people singing "Sweet Adeline." As Colt looked over the bat wings of the saloon, he surveyed the room, sizing up what he would be contending with. It looked like three farmers unarmed, two cowboys, armed, two soldiers, and four civilians, all armed, the bar tender who he presumed had the usual bar gun on a shelf, and four bar girls, two of whom were dancing with cowboys. The piano player and the fiddler and the harmonica player were the band.

As Colt pushed through the batwings a Waltz began, the hall was dark from poor lighting and many shadows were cast in all directions. Colt felt his targets were present from what the fat bartender said. Colt unbuttoned his long slicker, revealing his belt gun, hung his slicker behind the handle of his Remington, and stepped in. He was watched steadily by the roulette dealer until he reached the bar when the dapper dealer with arm bands, black string tie, realized he wasn't playing. He resumed paying attention to his two farmer customers. Colt ordered beer. He never drank whiskey when he thought he might have work to do. As he lifted his beer he was approached by a cute whore who came up, rubbed up against him, even brushed his crotch. With important things on his mind, he gave the girl a cold, disdainful look, even though he felt tremors of delight in his loins seeing he hadn't enjoyed any female company for awhile since he was laid up. She drew back with a sneer on her face. "The least you could of done was buy a girl a drink who's trying to welcome a stranger to town," she pouted.

When he gave her the cold deathlike stare he exhibited before he killed someone she felt the coldness, the anger and backed away.

He turned his head hearing, "My mercantile is the best stocked store this side of Denver, ask anyone, but that don't mean you don't pay me on time. Now I expect for you to tally up by the end of the month," he lectured his customer, a thin, tall man who appeared to be a farmer. Colt set his stein down, said to the bartender loud enough to be heard by Elias Connelly, "Excuse me bartender, I'm looking for Elias Connelly." The bearded bartender nodded towards the far table.

Elias, who was talking with his farmer customer hearing his name turned around, "At your service sir, mercantile goods, cattle bought and sold," smiling while he said it. He advanced toward Colt, leaned on the bar next to him. "Got anything you need, but it's cash only for out of towners. I can also sell you…"

"I came to find out about the man you hanged."

Elias Connelly laughed. "That was no man, it was a savage Indian."

"Oh, really, who did he scalp and kill?"

Half of the people in the dance hall heard the question and the answer. Several dancers stopped, the fiddler stopped and a minute later the piano player, then silence took over the hall except for low hushed whispers. Colt flashed a friendly smile to confuse his intentions until he was ready, reminding himself that the mustached bartender was behind him, more than likely with a scatter gun.

Elias laughed heartily, ignored the question. "We took care of that no good, stinking buck, let me tell you."

"Yes, I guess you did," and Colt nodded with a warm, wide smile so Elias would relax and not be on his guard. "Just wondering how it went down."

The deception worked. Elias waved to the bartender for a drink, turned back to Colt. "Why that impertinent savage came in demanding we produce a doctor for him. Now we told him in a nice way this was an establishment that didn't serve no stinkin' Indians, but he wouldn't leave. Would you believe the nerve of that Redskin?"

"You're saying he came in here for help trusting someone would give him some?"

"Yeh, the damn fool, he had more nerve than any Indian I ever saw. He looked like an Arapahoe to me with the kind of leggings he was sporting."

"He was Cheyenne."

Elias stopped his glass in mid air that he was going to sip and suddenly felt uneasy, beads of sweat appeared on his forehead, gradually sensing this was getting touchy.

Colt checked the room again, saw no threats stirring, resumed making this big blubbery mercantile, ranching killer sweat. It was a good feeling. "Oh, did you know the blanket head?" Colt had the entire dance hall listening carefully now and thought he would keep them guessing some more.

"Well, when I took a close look at him I could see he was Cheyenne, not an Arapahoe. Cheyenne are taller with narrower noses."

Colt noticed the mustached bartender edging over a few feet like he was getting nearer to a weapon he might have under the bar.

"You sure are perceptive mister, what business you in that you knew that?"

"Trapper. Tell me how the hanging went down."

Colt's mild voice again deceived the large man. He grimaced, "Well, it didn't take long, and we had a little sport with him before we strung him up."

"Oh, so you had sport with him before you strung him up, huh." Colt's right hand was twitching near his Remington. "Well, I'll let you know why he was here. I was laid up with pneumonia for a week almost dying, except for some settlers seeing me through and he was here trying to get me help."

"But – but, if you knew the injun why didn't you come out and say..."

"Because I wanted to hear it from you. You hung a good man, my partner."

Elias gulped, he didn't even see the swift draw, but he saw the hole of the Remington 44 looking at him. He gulped deeply a few times.

With a cold, steely, monotone he looked at the mustached bar keep, who had edged up to the bar where he kept his shotgun. "This is between us two, fat man. You would be advised to stay out of it."

"Why I..."

"Shut up and back away from the bar."

Colt then shot his eyes back to Elias. "I don't care if you did lose a sister-in-law to the Arapahoe. My friend didn't do it, you had no call to hang him. He was a fine decent man and I intend to kill you now."

"What! For a sleazy indi..."

The shot hit Elias in the forehead, interrupting his sentence.

Colt heard gasps in the crowd. Colt looked around the room and cautioned, "Now this concerns only LaTour and myself now, no one else."

Ed LaTour was sucking on his knuckles, "I didn't do anything, I didn't tie the knot, I didn't hit the horse," he whimpered.

"No, but you egged the others on, and you didn't stop it either."

"How could I?" then a stream of urine stained his pants.

Someone shouted, "You ain't going to shoot an unarmed man are you?"

Colt looked contemptuously at the man, reached in his belt, threw the Navy dragoon Colt down in front of LaTour. He just ignored it, shut his eyes and whimpered, "Please, I, I..." Colt's shot took him in the right shoulder, knocking him backwards collapsing in a heap. Colt walked over, picked up his Navy Colt, put it back in his belt, leaned over and saw that LaTour was still breathing. He shot him in the head, looked around the room at the stunned, shocked people, leisurely backed up and out the door, mounted, and waited outside the door a few minutes.

"Humph, no heroes here I guess." He swung aboard his horse, backed his horse up twenty feet, keeping the saloon door in full view, then turned, leisurely cantered down the single street out of town.

Fatal Beauty

When Carmella Binghampton was only nine years old and already beautiful, even then she created an aura of presence wherever she went. Her sister Elainie was twelve. They were both Binghamptons, yet were very different in many ways. Carmella had flaming red hair, Tessie dark brown, the usual hair color of a Binghampton. Carmella even at a young age displayed uniqueness and was noticed by friends and visitors wherever she went. At nine Carmella had the tint of voluptuousness that presaged future charm. She lived on a farm twenty miles from Beloit, Wisconsin, in the farming town of Alton. She worked hard, was a good daughter in many ways, but she hated the hard work, the scripted scheduling of chores. As she matured she knew more and more this was not the life for her. She craved the life she saw in the newspapers, magazines, on television, most of all she wanted excitement.

Her sister Elainie was a year older. Both girls were unmistakable Binghamptons, yet they contrasted in many ways. Only Carmella impressed people with her wit and captivating charm, while ordinary Elainie was more subdued and reconciled to the agricultural life. At social functions, dances, picnics, Carmella was sought after by boys. These triumphs were minor to Carmella, the things she wanted were not present in her farming community. The things she was seeking was not here, for some reason she wanted the anonymity that insulated you in a large city. Carmella tried to enlist her sister Elainie's interest in joining her adventurous, ambitious mission for social advancement, acquisition of a wealthy, successful man.

Elainie freely confided in Carmella that she thought Tom Appleton was the man for her.

"But Elainie," Carmella would say, "you could do so much better than a farmer. Look how ma weathered before her time. Farming is too hard on a woman Elainie, think of yourself a little will you?"

"Oh Carmella, you don't understand, do you? It's the animals, the things growing, the life, the country that I love, and I think I have a man who loves the serene life and the same things I do. It's what I want Carmella, don't you understand that? I love Tom with all my heart, don't you see?"

"No I don't, and I feel sorry for you Elainie, I truly do."

Carmella was convinced that anyone that pursued the agrarian life was suspect for having lack of motivation for higher achievements. She redoubled her efforts to dissuade her sister from developing her relationship with Tom Appleton. She continued to vilify him by stigmatizing him as a typical country bumpkin, slow witted, an idiot, failing to recognize his taciturnity as the caution of a man who spoke when he knew something for sure instead of commenting on undocumented facts. Tom Appleton's guarded comments were misleading, he was actually an astute man of solid character, consistent with steadfast qualities that one would appreciate if they took the time to be unbiased which Carmella certainly was not.

Elainie had long abandoned any hope of convincing Carmella of Tom Appleton's qualities, the one which she never mentioned was his dedicated devotion and unrequited declarations of love to her in word, action and deed.

The local adoration and social triumphs enjoyed in Alton were minor and inconsequential to Carmella. The things she wanted were not present in her farming community. Carmella Binghampton was filled with vivacity and voluptuousness, clever witted, ambitious with the selfish capacity to ignore convention, fairness, people's feelings, to cruise toward things she coveted. She had learned to use her femininity as a weapon over men long, long ago. Carmella was better equipped for survival in the city than most. She had learned long ago she could handle most any man. She always agreed with them, lowered her long lashes coyly in a modest maidenly gesture accidently revealing a fleeting glimpse of beautiful young, firm white cleavage, she operated with such smoothness the man never suspected he had been manipulated.

She flashed back to the time she discovered her power over men. Her first sexual experience was with Will Allen, a neighbor boy in the barn hayloft. She felt very little joy, not realizing that due to her bodily beauty, he was so excited he was premature, denying her any pleasure what so ever. She felt the other girls that told her it was fun were lying. She felt they lied to put her on because she didn't feel much of anything. Oh well, she thought the lack of pleasure was Will Allen's fault, not hers. She determined to experiment when an opportunity presented itself.

    Late that summer she visited her cousin in Beloit. In the downtown business district on a balmy Saturday night at seven o'clock she found herself walking on a nearly deserted street, when she heard a whistle, turned around and saw a rough hewn soldier, grinning. He was at least twenty years older. She joined him with eager expectations. They talked awhile, walked awhile, and despite her trepidation she consented to go to a dim tawdry looking bar on the edge of town. She was fearful someone would recognize her, but the feeling of doing the naughty and the forbidden overcame her hesitation, backing out now was out of the question.

Two blocks after they turned into the street from the saloon she looked into the general merchandise window of a Dollar Store they were passing by, noticing silken pillows, scarves, hats, trinkets, cheap jewelry, she suddenly got this thought in her mind. Looking up at the soldier, she brought up the subject, talked in and around it for awhile, but made it quite clear that the cost of a pair of pear shaped counterfeit pearl earrings were the price of her agreeability to his wishes. She was stunned when without a word he dashed headlong into the store and emerged a few minutes later holding the earrings. This important discovery excited Carmella, knowing that the sexual wants of men can weave a power over them. Having exhorted great satisfaction in her discovery, she found herself eagerly disrobing, but tense, taut, and when she saw him remove his shorts, she was both thrilled and frightened at the immense size of his erection but overall eager. She was rocketed into a succession of explosions, while groaning, whimpering, moaning, she had no idea that this activity was so much pleasure and also sensed it's great practical use for establishing influence over men.

    Carmella was dejected with her initial lack of success in the big city. She had no idea where to apply, or for what job she was capable to perform. After submitting a number of applications she was forced to take a menial job in a factory assembling transistors. It was monotonous and tedious work, the plant was dark, dismal with unclean working conditions. She quit as soon as she found a job making sandwiches at the 2nd Avenue Bainbridge Automat on Fifth and Washington. She didn't like this job either. There was no way to put her ambitious plan into operation. Being pretty, not being able to meet anyone of substance, soured her on this job too and demoralized her ego. This was not the opportunity she was seeking when she came to the big city. Nothing was working out like she planned.

    "How long you worked here May?" Carmella asked her coworker who was making salads alongside of her on the long work table.

    May stopped working, put one hand on her hip, leaned her elbow on the counter,

Ten Stories of Mystery – Suspense – Adventure – Intrigue

"Honey, I had the best damn job I ever had working at the ritzy Commerce Club with the Hoi Poloi and, Honey, if I was younger and had your looks I'd still be at the Commerce Club where the guys with the bucks are," she paused, "yeah the Commerce Club was where I made money, had more good times than I ever had before or since."

"Why did you leave if it was so good?"

"Honey, if I had your looks, I'd still be there, but I fell out of demand with the members. When that happens the girls are gone and new ones are hired."

"I don't understand it May."

"Ya don't huh? Well if the guys like you, the money you make is unbelievable. Sometimes if they really like you, you really cash in. I had my day there and I don't mind telling you if I had your looks I would have done a hell of a lot better than I did. Out of respect for myself I won't say any more."

Carmella thought she understood May's tacit description of the activities at the exclusive Commerce Club and her adventuresome curiosity was whetted. Carmella was intrigued with the Commerce Club and possibilities that May described. Actually it was more in line with what she had in mind even before she came to Milwaukee, she just didn't know where to look. Carmella and May talked about the Commerce Club a little each day.

"You could make it there Hon, I know it. Why not give it a try? This job sure ain't holding you, that's for sure."

The constant urging and encouragement from May added to her wish to elevate herself prompting Carmella to switch days and get a Monday off from the automat. Her interview and employment was swift thanks to the coaching she received from May. When she was asked how much experience she had, she said, "Oh, I worked in a catering company for a while," then she recounted how she worked in a diner in Madison for a while.

"Well, it's not the level of experience exactly, that were looking for."

Despite his comment Carmella felt she was near acceptance from the reaction, nuances of Mr. Samson's behavior. She knew men liked to look at her and she felt from the telltale signs Mr. Samson was no exception. Oh, he was professional alright, but she had seen the reactions underneath his comments and the looks that he gave her that restored the smug feeling there was no man she couldn't influence if she had the opportunity.

Carmella found no difficulty in adjusting to the requirements of the job. Most of the members of the Commerce Club were older men, well to do, most bordering on rich. They dressed elegantly, gambled for large sums of money and were generous tippers. The third week she was requested often by Dr. Wanstadt, Mr. Eagleton, and Mr. Holleck. Carmella was elated, all three proved to be generous tippers. Dr. Wanstadt and Mr. Eagleton were businesslike and were easy to please, they enjoyed the pleasant, sparkling girl. They were gentlemen, never varying from proper decorum and always speaking to her as a worthy individual despite her service occupation. She found it hard to place them on her enemies list of no good men. Holleck on the other hand engaged Carmella in long conversations, off color jokes which she feigned lack of appreciation. She didn't mind his crude efforts to debase her because he tipped well. She also felt that he was coming on to her and was delighted that it was happening, after all that was in the back of her mind ever since she came to town.

Holleck was senior vice president and large stock holder of the Halleger Gear Company. He was a widower five years now. He had a daughter and two lovely grandchildren who lived in San Francisco, California. He never saw his grandchildren or his daughter in ten years. His daughter Janet despised him for his infidelity. She felt his cheating on her mother was a factor in her dying so young. She even refused to take his calls. Holleck was a selfish man used to getting his way one way of another. He spent a lot of time at the Commerce Club. It had the best food, he played poker with other members, chess, and used his position at the club to prey on the young girls waiting on the members using temptations that would corrupt struggling girls. The girls who were playful became known, then systematically seduced with tips, bribes and gifts. When their novelty was exhausted they were found lacking in their duties by management who bowed to the requests of the few but influential lascivious members' demands and promptly replaced.

Holleck was pleased with the, attractive new attendant that graced the dining room and the club and with his usual crudeness to a few close pals said, "I think she'll be easy." He said to one pal to another making lewd comments about what he wished her to do for him. His reputation was as a boaster, a boorish man who was not the least egalitarian but elitist in his thinking, behavior, and treatment of those less fortunate than himself, linking his estimation and esteem, corresponding to their occupations. With this standard his attitude toward Carmella was that she was a nobody, not too well fixed and would be susceptible to his advances for pocket change. He never got involved emotionally and more than once cruelly dropped a girl without notice.

Carmella knew Holleck was exhibiting interest in her and she was determined to handle the situation just right.

In several ensuing conversations, Holleck initially casually invited her for dinner at his posh condominium on the lake front. He loved to dazzle the girls with its opulence. Once he was able to seduce a young girl just from her awed impression of its splendor.

"Oh Mr. Holleck," Carmella would answer, "I really couldn't." She never said no, just gave solid reasons, like I have to check on my mother, I'm dinning with my sister's family tonight, or I have a doctor's appointment.

Mr. Holleck's desire grew proportionately to the length and time of her unavailability. After a number of rejections, Mr. Holleck regressed to asking her to join him in courteous tones for dinner in exclusive restaurants, in downtown Milwaukee, but she repeatedly offered an apparently valid reason why she couldn't.

Mr. Holleck was agitated, accustomed to being accommodated instead of rebuffed. He thought he would try something different. One evening when Carmella had finished taking his order for dinner he raised a small box with a white ribbon tied around it and said condescendingly in a gruff voice, "This is for you," then he smiled a sharkish smile, like a hungry animal waiting to be fed.

Carmella was disdainful of Holleck's pompous, patronizing, haughty attitude when he offered her the gift, she vowed to herself that this supercilious, pompous ass would be brought down hard. She detested superior, imperious men. They reminded her of her mother's unhappy life. "Oh, my goodness," she smiled sweetly. "That's really nice of you Mr. Holleck, but I can't accept that, it wouldn't be proper, but I am most appreciative of the thought sir." She smiled, turned around and walked away with her most provocative sway feeling Holleck's hungry eyes on her as she walked away.

The other girls gossiped a great deal. Through conversation Carmella learned one of the richest members and one of the most depraved was Holleck, but they said, "He sure as hell pays off if he likes you, but when the bastard tires of you though, he drops you like a hot coal." Carmella smiled to herself. No man she was personal with ever got enough of her.

Mr. Holleck was seventy-two years old. Bald except for a fringe of hair from ear to ear. wore black horn rimmed glasses, wide mouth with thick lips, resembling a guppy. He was medium height, with a rounded paunch in front. He had ears that were pointy and stood out from his head. He was not a handsome man and with his crude demanding behavior he was not appealing to women. He was a selfish lover, only concerned with his gratification. His only relationship with women developed from a campaign of allurement and seduction with gifts, promises and money. Without these lures Mr. Holleck would have had to resort to common whores for the fulfillment of his feeble sexual whims.

Mr. Holleck from frustration abandoned his tactic of risqué comments, disregard for her personage and adopted a new gentler course of action. His addressees were now respectful, he eliminated the coarse suggestions and jokes and tried to be pleasant. He wanted to get to know Carmella. He enjoyed their brief exchanges at meal time at the Commerce Club and he wished to see more of her.

One evening after Carmella had placed his London Broil, asparagus, and baked potato in front of him, he asked in a respectful tone, "Carmella, have you by any chance seen the play, "South Pacific" at the Palace Theatre?"

"No Mr. Holleck, I have not. I wanted too but it's not in my budget right now." She had chosen her reply with the intention of baiting him, feeling he was prepared for the next phase of his orientation.

"Well then, that's it," he said. "I haven't seen it either. Would you do me the honor of accompanying me to dinner at Manganno's and then see the show? I would be very pleased."

Carmella was amused at his subdued manner in contrast with his former discourteous, superior, arrogant behavior. "Why, I believe I would like to see that play very much."

Holleck was elated he finally, after several months, obtained a social engagement with Carmella. He felt he finally was getting where he wanted to go with her.

Carmella was smirking to herself. So far she had transformed Holleck from an ill mannered boor who didn't respect her to a careful talking man who pleaded repeatedly for a date with her. She disliked Holleck, whom she felt was the despicable type of a man that deserved every humiliation that a woman could inflict on him.

Her poise, appearance and the sly glances, and quick peeks she generated from men in the theatre crowd impressed Holleck and confirmed his earlier opinion that Carmella Binghamton was indeed something extraordinary, which inflamed his expectations anew, but with greater intensity. He wasn't used to patience or being put off by a woman, but he sensed if he was impetuous and demanding she would again refuse him and this he didn't want to happen. He didn't admit it to himself, but he was quite smitten with Carmella and the weirdest thing about it Holleck mused, was he was never even personal with her yet, not even a kiss.

Three weeks later, after several more social outings, Al Holleck had become more and more enamored with Carmella. She kept him in a state of wanting. When she thought he needed a reminder of things to come, after an evening out when he brought her home, she would allow him to kiss her at her door, carelessly allowing her hand to drop down and brush his groin, smiling to herself when she detected his reaction, then murmuring, "Oh Al, you affect me so," leaving him in a tense, aroused state with an unsatisfied appetite for more, and a greater desire to see Carmella again.

Holleck, stricken with desire for Carmella and being an astute and experienced observer of human behavior, had a flashing sense he was being manipulated, but she did it with such degrees of finesse that he really wasn't convinced of it and preferred to reject the idea. Nothing she did was obvious or blatant that he could make an issue out of, so he was just drawn further and further into Carmella's web of influence. His desire was deep enough that he kept convincing himself that she was just a nice, moral, small town girl which accelerated his plans for them.

One evening after they watched the Chicago Bulls play in Milwaukee he took Carmella's hand after dinner and said, "Carmella, I want you to share my condominium. I would find it most desirable." He produced a velvet case. "Would you do me the pleasure of putting these on?" He opened the case, displaying a magnificent string of flawless pearls.

Carmella, always poised an collected, casually, masking her joy at such a lovely gift, intentionally without a great deal of enthusiasm to maintain a degree of independence, without any promises, said, "Thank you Al, they're nice, but I won't say a yes or no on any sharing right now." If you still wish, I'll put them on as soon as I'm finished with my chocolate Mousse cake." Finishing her chocolate Mousse, she continued, "Al, I won't move in with you. It's too far from work, too inconvenient."

Holleck smiled, his thick guppy-like lips stretched over his yellow teeth, said, "That won't be a problem. I want you to quit work, just shop all day and tend to me and my condominium. We'll be happy."

"Oh Al, that is sweet of you but I'll have to think that over for a while." She had to recruit all of her poise and control to conceal her delight in getting Al Holleck to do what she wanted him to do all the time.

Carmella stalled a week, suppressing her excitement, then tentatively informed Al Holleck that she might if she felt he really thought enough of her because, she said, "If you don't have deep feelings for me I just couldn't bring myself to it, thinking my affection for you was not shared."

Holleck was so delighted to hear this he leaped up, embraced Carmella, pressing her firm bosom against his panting chest and blubbered, "Carmella, I not only have deep feelings for you, I am falling in love with you."

Carmella exhibited a surprised, happy look and gently pressed her lips to his. Carmella smiled to herself. The request came from Holleck, she had the intention to move in the first time she saw the palatial, luxurious penthouse condominium and now she was here, things were working out just like she planned. He was being manipulated just as she planned.

Holleck never complained about the money she spent, never asked her where she went during the day, just wanted her there when he came home. Carmella acceded to his every request the first few months. His inept, fumbling, inadequate love making was disgusting to Carmella. She actually disliked even touching his ugly wrinkled body, but she was accumulating money and jewelry and felt pleased with her progress. It was worth it. The first six months everything was new, she wasn't bored, she was squirreling money away every week which was her plan. Holleck was happy, he gave parties, dinners, often, just to display the lovely Carmella. He was a contented man.

At a birthday party in January she greeted Ted Wilson and his wife Anne, the

Gailsons, the Gordons, and the Carpenters. All were directors of the Seebring Corporation who also golfed together. It was a lovely evening. When the guests left, Holleck said, "Carmella, you were the perfect hostess, your wit, charm and management of the entire affair was flawless, you're a real refined woman my love."

The combination of a perfect evening of sociability, the meeting with the tall, strapping, handsome Jon Carpenter plus the effusive compliments of Holleck gave Carmella an unexpected sexual arousal. In bed Holleck was huffing and puffing, sweating and laboring as he struggled to make love to her. Many times in the last six months she told him how inadequate he was. Gasping from his exertion he whispered, "Was it ok this time?"

"Yes, just fine," she lied.

Quite often in the early evening Holleck would go over where Carmella was sitting reading, reach over and attempt to fondle her. She would slap his hand away like he was a little boy. Without looking up she would say, "Don't bother me now," dismissing him.

Disappointed, Holleck would sulk and move away. "Why do you treat me this way

Ten Stories of Mystery – Suspense – Adventure – Intrigue

Carmella? Is it because we aren't married yet? Just because I've been weak and gave in to you doesn't mean I will stand for this treatment for ever you know. I should have some privileges," he complained.

"Well yes, but not just now, and I don't feel like arguing about it either."

"Is this the way you intend to act if I decided to marry you?"

"Well," she laughed, "you'll just have to wait and see now won't you?"

Al Holleck was slowly crafting the whole picture. If he married her it would be on her terms. The poor fool sensed it, but in effect had already surrendered and embraced the idea.

A week later the air was chilled, snow was on the ground, Milwaukee sparkled with blinking, colored lights in the decorated store windows and on the evergreen trees in the parkway. Carmella exited the cab in front of busy Nordstroms, spent an hour purchasing a few gifts, then as dusk was coming on she was exiting the revolving door when she was jolted against the glass door, dropping her packages. "Oh, I'm so sorry," the man said as he took her elbow and helped her to her feet. "Oh, for gosh sakes, it's you Carmella. Please forgive my awkwardness, I'm so sorry."

Carmella looked at Jon Carpenter, trying to look unaffected and nonchalant by his masculine looking virility. She was so in need of a man, it was only with great difficulty she was able to keep her poise.

"Carmella, I was just on my way to lunch. Please join me. You know, make it up to you for knocking you down."

Carmella made a decision at that moment. She needed more in her life than the decrepit, wrinkled, frail Holleck. Jon Carpenter was a faithful married man who never thought about an extra marital affair, but when Carmella unleashed her arsenal of charms and cast out vibes on her accessibility he found himself in a torrid romance meeting her twice week at the Hilton Hotel on Washington Avenue. Jon Carpenter fell hard for this woman that seemed to be perfect in every way. She launched into the affair succumbing to her wild pent up urge to take a man, then this handsome, rich man came along and she reached for him. She always felt she could entice any man she really wanted, but she still observed her number one rule, "never fall in love with a man." She wanted to be the one in charge. She knew if this affair got out she would be out with Holleck, but then realized that Jon Carpenter inflamed and gave her what she craved. She was a fulfilled woman now, and as their affair progressed, Jon brought up some discussion of a future together.

The last tryst they had Jon said, "You know Carmella you're really something."

"You mean you have no regrets meeting me?"

"No way, I think you're just about the best I ever had."

Carmella puckered up her lips in mock protest, "What, what do you mean just about the best?"

He leaned over and kissed her taut, firm white breast, "You're a conceited tart too, ok," then laughed. "You're the best." He looked at her engaging lovely face, flawless nude body with awe, "My God Carmella, you're something."

Carmella reflected what a fine lover Jon was, he met her whenever she called, but if she didn't call he didn't come. It bothered her, but when he was with her he was so attentive, so pleasing, he always left her exhausted. She had a flashing thought one day, "What if he had others too? Well so what," she thought, they couldn't compare to her. He comes when I call doesn't he? That was reassurance enough for her.

The following Tuesday as they were leaving the hotel Carmella cooed, "Oh, John, I'm so happy, I never knew I could feel so wonderful. I wish we could be together all the time, not like this."

"Yes, I know, I know," he said as he covered both her hands in his, leaned forward slightly and kissed her lightly. "It won't be much longer, I promise. I will tell her soon."

Jon hated to leave Carmella feeling vulnerable and uneasy whenever she wasn't with him. He knew he was slightly paranoid about her, but he couldn't help himself, he felt so in love with her. He marveled at how fortunate he was to have found such a sweet, sincere girl who wasn't the least interested in material things, but enjoyed the art institute, the science museum, opera, a play, the exact things he enjoyed. It seemed like whenever he expressed an interest in something, she also had the interest. Their compatibility surprised him, but pleased him very much.

Jon Carpenter was executive vice president of Marble Mayfield, manufacturers of counter tops, vanity tops, tile, both floor and wall, with stores in twenty-five cities in the East and the South, lived in a million dollar home, three cars and a summer home.

On his drive home to his suburban home in fashionable Barrington, Illinois he reflected on the happiness he would enjoy with Carmella Binghampton. His mind swirled up and away when he thought about how wonderful their life together would be with her. He exalted when they walked together, how other men turned their heads for a glimpse of this exceptional woman, and was comfortable with her non reaction to the attention she commanded. He accorded this to attributes of breeding, education, being a lady and goodness to Carmella all traits that his wife Lilla possessed that caused him to fall in love with her their first year in college. Meeting someone with all those wonderful traits plus such fantastic looks made him feel like he was charmed.

Arriving home after midnight, he unlocked the front door went in. Lilla Carpenter was his wife of fifteen years, was his college sweetheart, worked to get him through his MBA until their two children were out of grammar school. She was sitting reading Elle when she heard the key turn and her husband enter the vestibule. "Well, Romeo, I guess you were out with that whore again, huh? You never come near me anymore, you never touch me anymore. What have I got, a contagious disease or something?"

"Lilla, please, can't you show some dignity and self respect? It's not like you to talk that way."

"Maybe not, but it's not easy having to watch your husband running around with a tramp either and expecting me to show refined manners when I talk about it." Jon had been sleeping in a separate bedroom for a year now.

"Lilla, it's over with us, can't you see that? It isn't fair to you to not let you get on with your life, and to me too, to get along with mine."

"Really Jon, why is it when a man cheats, runs out on his wife and children, he's always doing the wife a favor? You're really a bastard Jon."

Jon shook his head in despair. He couldn't think of anything appropriate to say to this woman that was loyal and true all the years of their married life. Doing what he was doing caused him deep grief and shame, however he knew Lilla would never be gracious or cooperative to make the dissolution of their marriage a reality, and didn't blame her. He made no response to her diatribe. What could he say in his defense anyway? Then with a guilty feeling slowly went up the stairs to his separate bedroom, hearing a muffled, "Oh Jon, you're such a fool," as he shut his door.

Carmella felt she had succeeded in her climb to her present position, and the most savory aspect of her progress was the use and abuse of men along the way. She smugly complimented herself on her euthanizing of the individuality of Holleck and Carpenter. They each did her bidding, not necessarily servile, but certainly under her whimsical requirements.

On Friday evenings Holleck usually spent a few hours at the club playing cards or chess, tonight he was a little longer. Carmella was glad when he was away, her packing was complete and she had her things picked up an hour ago, she intended to leave a note, but now he was coming in earlier than usual. She had come to detest his very presence and made no efforts to hide her scorn. She had been denying him personal favors now for several weeks despite Holleck's pleadings and mild protests. She heard the door close, looked up at a smiling Holleck.

"Hello dear," he said, and went over to kiss her.

"Oh, don't," Carmella said in an admonitory tone. "I just put make up on." Then she said, lying, "I'm glad you're home, I was just ready to leave."

"What? It's almost nine o'clock, where are you going?"

With a cruel satisfying curl to her mouth she said, "I'm leaving you Al." She delighted in saying this, knowing he had done this to more than one girl before. Well, she was doing it to him, let's see how he will handle it. This was a moment she looked forward to since the first time Holleck treated her with such insulting condescension at the Commerce Club. She had intended to just leave a note, but him coming home early gave her this unexpected pleasure to tell him personally.

Ten Stories of Mystery – Suspense – Adventure – Intrigue

Holleck had suspected for the last few months Carmella was being unfaithful as she became colder, less courteous, less agreeable, starting an argument on the slightest pretense. He sensed something was happening, but he didn't know what. He was so fearful of losing her he avoided confronting her. Holleck stood with his mouth agape. "Leaving, what are saying?"

"Al, I am leaving tonight. Things are not working our here for me at all."

"What are you talking about Carmella? What's got into you? What's wrong? What have I done wrong?"

Carmella laughed, "What have you done wrong? The question is, what have you done right?" She laughed a mocking, taunting laugh of ridicule. This was sweeter than she could have imagined.

"Now, now," he slurred, "let's talk about this. I've been good to you, I've got a right to know. Please, let's talk about it, you're making a mistake."

Carmella was enjoying seeing him come apart by degrees. "The only right you have you old coot is to know what I think of you."

With tears in his eyes, he pleaded, "Please, whatever is bothering you, I can fix. Please, change your mind. Why, I'll even marry you, we'll get married immediately."

Carmella sneered at his condescending offer and felt insulted that he would think an offer of marriage from him was any kind of inducement at all. "Ha, really, why I wouldn't marry an old broken down guy like you. Marriage to you would be a purgatory, you stink, have bad breath, can't do anything in bed worthwhile. Are you kidding?"

The impending loss of Carmella was crushing enough, but to hear her loathing opinion of him, stripped him of his ego, self esteem, rendered him bare, shamed him, with a vacuous feeling of total defeat. This was the bitterest experience of his life, and was at a time when he was least able physically to endure it. He clutched his heart momentarily then covered his face with two hands, muffling, "Stop it, stop it!" With tears streaming down his face Holleck sunk down to the floor sobbing. Carmella felt no pity, thinking of his insulting treatment of her when she started work at the Commerce Club. She vowed then she would make him pay for his patronizing, superior behavior, belittling attitude like she was less worthy and in a lower class. Oh, she admitted he treated her courteously and generously now, but from a perspective of always looking down at her. Well now as she was looking down at him babbling, weeping, she felt exhilarated and refreshed, totally dominant. She stepped around him and slammed the door behind her.

"I heard at the club this evening that Holleck had a stroke, night before last, the night you left him. Did you know that?"

Carmella, with a puzzled look of innocence, shook her head, "Goodness no, he was fine when I last saw him."

"It must have been a shock to him Carmella, poor guy."

"Well, he never was real hardy Jon, I'm not surprised, but I am sorry," she lied. She had hated Holleck with a passion and wasn't the least disturbed he was ailing.

Sunday afternoon when Jon called the convalescent center he was bluntly told, "Don't ever speak to me again."

Jon knew Holleck blamed him for Carmella leaving him, but he suggested Carmella call anyway to see how he was getting along.

Carmella was watching the news. Without turning her head she said, "No, I don't care how he is. He was an insufferable tyrant and I don't pity him at all."

Jon turned to look at Carmella, noting the lack of feeling and finding the incident so incompatible with her exaggerated expressions of compassion and pity for his wife, for him when he encountered some scheduling problem or an announcement of a challenging situation at work. It was the first flag that caught his notice in his perfect, beautiful live in bride to be. It was a display of lack of compassion that was incongruous with a kindly nature she exhibited up to now, and it bothered him to see it.

Though Jon was expecting separation papers from Lilla's attorney, a mutual friend of them both, it did nothing to neutralize the discomfiture he felt when he read the document.

He and Carmella were living in an elegant high-rise on Milwaukee's northern edge on the lake. Their accommodations were all that Carmella could have hoped for and a man whom she admired to share it with. Well she concluded now that's done, I can pursue my usual plans with Jon Carpenter. Her compulsive desire to dominate every man began immediately in many ways.

While Jon was desirable to her he escaped her usual dedicated mission of vendetta against men, after all, he qualified for acceptance in many ways, handsome, well off, a viral, pleasing lover. Now to complete her happiness, when her dominance was complete she would be a content woman. Her resolve was that no man would gain control over her like her father did to her mother, no, she would be in charge.

The subconscious comparisons between Carmella and Lilla began creeping into Jon's mind from time to time. He noticed after a few months, Carmella was no longer tending to the details of his convenience, like a home cooked meal which he had become accustomed to. Oh, when they rendezvoused for their illicit trysts she made him a fine dinner every time, now failed to make a dinner one time and she no longer made a display of providing his robe and slippers, which didn't bother him, but the subtle changes collectively he observed was a little disturbing. He ignored the signs, wanting her availability and enjoying her romantic artistry. After a few weeks he was rebuffed as often as he engaged her in bed. He also noticed for the first time whimsical behavior, which bothered him. Lilla was just the opposite, he could always count on her. Not realizing that he was denied, with the motive of reducing him to begging, he began reflecting on his wife of fifteen years who never was in denial, but an agreeable, accommodating mate at all times. As the contest between Jon and Carmella unfolded, his eventual indifference to her denials miffed her and the initiative shifted as Carmella began to understand that Jon Carpenter was a rock of a man, a good man, uncomplicated, pure of heart and actions and that she was fortunate to have a man like that. But, she pondered, where is my control of this man? Why am I not exercising dominance over him? All I want to do is to be in charge, that's all, she thought.

She began thinking too that in the beginning she had a difficult time fending Jon off, he couldn't get enough of her which was exactly part of her scheme for domination, but when she attempted to disappoint him to try and capitalize on his want it didn't happen.

Carmella had never met a man like Jon before. He actually resisted vying for sexual activity unless she made overtures. She couldn't understand it. Was something going wrong? Was this a man she couldn't dominate? As this realization dawned on her that Jon Carpenter could survive with his independence, his sense of well being intact and not be reduced to a man enthralled with desire for her that would compromise his self respect and resort to entreaties for attention, she suddenly realized that without that victory she felt vulnerable and insecure. The feeling of losing control brought on tears. She despised her weakness, but did lessen her aggressive campaign to achieve superiority. She wouldn't admit it to herself, but even though she changed in attitude, Jon seemed to change too, it wasn't the same now with him. Now Carmella was the one who reached out to him, was a readily eager bed time companion, but his desire and responses were not with the same fervor and intensity or frequency as before, in fact, he actually denied her on occasion, something that no man ever did to her before.

    Carmella was getting frustrated. She never met a man who exerted such immunity to her charms, she never encountered a man who possessed the quiet strength and strong, confident persona that Jon possessed. This troubled her. She needed reassurance.

"Jon, when will you be divorced so we can be married" she would ask.

"Oh, it's moving along. You know how slow those lawyers are, the longer they string it out, the more fees they earn."

Actually Jon was not pressing the attorneys for completion. He had developed misgivings about what had happened to him and was flooded with conflicting thoughts about what he was losing, his children, a stable happy family, a loyal, attractive wife who temporarily lost her luster in his eyes when an opportunity for an affair with a beautiful woman came along. He now realized after his involvement with Carmella that a magnificent body and an affair are hardly compensation for the upheaval of an ideal home life. He had time to assess the traits of Carmella, and Lilla and realized his wife was a woman with superb character, steadfastness, a wonderful mother, a fine mate and he was misguided in what he was doing. He began thinking about how he could gracefully withdraw from his relationship with Carmella.

Ten Stories of Mystery – Suspense – Adventure – Intrigue

On Thursday afternoon at 3:00, Jon left his office, swept by his former home, not once but several times drove around the upscale homes, the manicured green well tended lawns, the flower beds of Azaleas, the trimmed hedges and trees. Twilight came on rapidly. He glanced toward the clouds that picked up the slanting lights from downtown and he parked on a hill top not too far from his former home. A panorama paraded before his eyes of family birthday parties, barbecues, family visitations, friends, his daughter Evy, at her joyous hugging of him when he had brought her the new bicycle that she wanted so much. He had his hands on the steering wheel with his head lowered in meditation about what he should do, and suddenly he saw everything clearly in his mind. While still gripping the steering wheel he began nodding his head up and down.

On Friday morning Jon's head was clear, he was resolved to correct his horrible error in judgment.

Carmella was ecstatic. Before Jon left for the office he invited her to meet him for lunch at the Commodore Hotel in room 510 on Main Street and Fifth Avenue to discuss something important. She was elated, their impending marriage was probably going to be the surprise, and they would have a romantic celebration like they used to, she thought. Why else would they meet in a hotel room? The bleak dismal rain peppered the cab as Carmella neared the Commodore Hotel. The rain had created a virtual lake with water up and over the sidewalk. Carmella exited the cab and sloshed to the entrance, refusing to allow the rain or her wet shoes to dampen her glow of expectation of the good news Jon was going to share with her.

"Ah, Carmella," Jon rose, took her coat, pulled a chair out for her.

"Thank you dear," she turned, kissed him on the cheek. "Oh what a grand idea Jon." The table was draped in a fine white linen table cloth, a vase of daffodils, fine china, and silver ware. The waiter brought, oysters, stuffed mushrooms, chicken soup, fine slabs of tasty lamb, mashed potatoes, several garnishments, the desert was cheese cake and coffee, but Carmella opted for tea which she thought was considerate of Jon to remember.

They had engaged in small talk throughout the luncheon. When they were finished Carmella smiled, "Well darling, all this was wonderful, now please tell me the good news. I can hardly contain myself, please."

Jon, grimaced, solemnly said, "Carmella, this is hard for me. You're a wonderful person and have been good in every way," he lied, "but I must tell you this, and I think it is best for both of us."

Carmella's quick mind alerted her. "What, what's going on here, huh?"

"Listen, what I'm trying to say is this won't work. I can't go through with this. I'm sorry, I just can't give up my family." What he didn't say was that he saw too many things in her metamorphosis from a sweet, agreeable, ever pleasing person into a selfish, domineering one and this added to everything else had helped dictate his decision.

Carmella saw everything she hoped and planned for disappearing in a flash before her eyes. She still wouldn't admit it to herself, but she had fallen in love with Jon Carpenter, violating her first rule for dealing with men. What she felt for him first was a longing, then anxiety, then that dissipated and melted into urgency. A rising passion began clouding her rational thinking and did away with her fears of exposing herself. Her mouth and hands were suddenly dry and her brain sizzled with hateful thoughts as it lifted her into a blind fury that surpassed anything she ever experienced before. Carmella staggered up, "No, no, you can't." She fingered her tea cup, flinging it and crashing it into the mirror, seized the vase with two hands, hurled it at the thermo pane window not breaking it, but causing a long crack near the bottom. She overturned the table, spilling dishes, food, drink, screaming all the while shouting at the top of her voice, "You lousy, bastard! You son of a bitch you!" She ran around the room, turning chairs over, ran into the bedroom and with a herculean effort turned over the bed, sobbing in disbelief that a man had spurned her. Actually she still didn't admit to herself her behavior was not so much being denied marriage as it was losing the only man she ever loved. She would never admit this. Jon had mumbled how sorry he was and had slipped out into the hallway leaving the door open in his haste.

The tenants, hearing the noise and destruction, called security who came up to confront Carmella who was still belligerent and fuming. When threatened with arrest, she calmed down and offered to pay for all damages which satisfied the hotel director.

Holleck with the able assistance of Captain Rodiquez and his attorney had put together the facts that Holleck intended to use to destroy her. She had been forced to leave the condominium after the month's rent that Jon paid had expired. She still had money and took a suitable apartment off Violet Street in a modest neighborhood. She did nothing but brood for several days. It was 10:00 o'clock when the sharp rap on her door shook her out of her sleep. She wrapped a robe around herself, opened the door, a hand thrust out, "Mam, you have been legally served."

The law suit claimed and won all the jewelry Holleck gave her restored to Holleck, unpaid rent on the condominium she shared with Holleck was declared unpaid and a monetary judgment was declared against her, if unpaid or failure to make an arrangement for payments were not made in 60 days she would be arrested for failure to obey a court order.

Ten days later the investigation that Rodriguez conducted into her background unearthed the two weeks that she earned quick money in an illicit activity. She was charged and thrown in jail. Her attorney assured her she would be out in the morning. In her lonely black barred cell, with a cot, toilet, a wash basin, she thought of the green fields of her home on the farm in Alton, her childhood, her mother, her sister, she thought about how she had so many advantages over most others and what good did it do for her? She thought about her amazing successes with men, but the thing she found unendurable was the loss of the only man she ever loved. She then looked around with deep depression. This added to the wails and cries and noise far into the night mounted her dread and doubt of the future. When they found her hanging by the neck with her skirt and blouse ripped and tied together, fastened to the window bars, it only earned two short lines in the Milwaukee Sentinel.

Grasping For a Fortune

The unkempt young man lazing on the lower bunk in cell three of the Cairo city Police Department was Chill Leonard. He was short, almost chinless, his pockmarked face, narrow shoulders, spare frame, with an unfriendly antisocial personality, identified him as a struggling loser. Although he was in a 6x10 cell, he was amused and laughing to himself thinking how he would have the last laugh on the Cairo city Police Department. He thought over what he, Trig Lamont, Bittle Remington and Shalop Rhodes did just a few days ago, and again was amused at how he was fooling the Cairo Police Department. The robbery of Bank One in Akron, Ohio took place on Thursday the 7th of June. When Trig Lamont, Bittle Remington, Shalop Rhodes fled the bank with the money, they leaped into the souped up fifty nine Chevy driven by Chill Leonard. The gang knew from monitoring their police scanner that road blocks were being hastily established and an APB was issued for three men with sketchy descriptions of them. The police acted so fast Trig knew a change of plan was necessary if they were to elude the police.

Trig Lamont had Chill pull up to the curb near a busy intersection in Akron outside a Walgreens with bustling traffic coming and going. Thinking fast, he said, "Boys, we gotta change plans fast. They'll be lookin' for three guys in a car. We know a single guy's got a better chance. Now Chill here lives over Maximo way about a hundred miles. He'll have the best chance of getting through with the money, he knows all the side roads, short cuts, crossings in the area. Instead of us heading down to Bittle's place in Canton for the split up we'll let Chill bury it on his folks' place, then we'll come up in a few weeks when the heat's off and split up. It's our best chance."

"Well, I don't know about that," said Shalop Rhodes.

"Me either," complained Bittle Remington. "I think I'd rather split the money up now."

"You're right, you dummies don't know, so shut up!" Trig yelled. "Every second we're here together we could be spotted. Now Chill, you take off with the money and the car now, bury it on that farm of yours. I'll contact you in a week or so and the boys and I will meet up with you for the split." Trig Lamont's eye's narrowed to slits, his eyes were cold and unforgiving. "If anything happens to that dough Chill," then he paused, "well you know what'll happen, don't you?"

Chill felt cold and clammy, he had never seen such a side to Trig Lamont as he saw now. He acted like the cautionary threat wasn't needed. "Got ya, Trig, don't worry, I'll take care of it," and he pulled away from the curb heading south.

Trig, Bittle and Shalop watched Chill start off at a casual pace so as not to attract any attention. Using secondary roads, little used cutoffs, roads known only to lifetime residents like himself, he was able several hours later to arrive safely in Maximo. He arrived at six at night, pulled into the family barn, used only for garaging the three vehicles of the Leonard family. Ma and Pa Leonard drove a ten year old pickup. Evalina, his older sister, drove a four year old Dodge and Chill was in his eight year old

Chevy which was selected to be used for the job because it was a souped up car that Chill had worked on constantly and was selected by Trig as the car to use for that reason. The farm was in the Leonard family for three generations. When Chill rebelled after leaving school and refused to farm, Ma and Pa Leonard sold the live stock, the machinery, retired, rented out the land to their neighbor, Ed Lanson, for nine hundred dollars a year.

Chill took the money bag, an elongated grey canvas bag, from the trunk of the car with black stenciled letters on it, "BANK ONE OF AKRON," and with a heave put it on his shoulder, grabbed a shovel against the barn wall, went outside away from view of the house and the road, walked two miles, just a short ways onto the next property that used to be owned by the Granger family who sold it off to the agri giant, Monsalvo Hybrid Seed Company. Chill Leonard looked at his father's fields and the farm next door that was owned by the Granger family for generations. He remembered as he was growing up the lush green rows of green corn, each year waving in the soft summer breezes and thought of how he used to lay

Ten Stories of Mystery – Suspense – Adventure – Intrigue

here in the shade of that big oak tree as it cast its shadow, the quiet and the peacefulness was something he always remembered. There were rumors all year long that the new owners of the Granger land were going to construct a huge plant on the site but they never followed through and the land had been rented out each year for crops to a local farmer who just harvested the corn a few weeks ago.

Chill Leonard didn't want to hide the money on his folks' place, if they arrested him and the money was found he didn't want it found on his folks' place and make them unknown and innocent accessories to bank robbery. He walked to the property line, went over to the fence line where about fifteen feet in a tall old gnarled oak poked skyward. Ten paces from the oak tree put him in the third row of the harvested former Granger corn field, where he decided to bury the money. He unzipped the huge money bag, plunged his hand into the bag. No way he thought would anyone dream what was buried here. He gripped five bundles of hundred dollar packets of bills with wrappers printed with BANK ONE AKRON, OHIO, stuffed them in his shirt, rezipped the bag, dug a hole five feet down in the soft fertile loose soil, shoveled the dirt back on top, then smoothed the surface with his hands making it look like it was never disturbed. Chill Leonard, still on his knees, started laughing hysterically, rolling on the ground, yahooing and laughing hysterically stunned at his big strike. With tears of joy in his eyes he headed for the farm house and supper.

    Chill Leonard had tried from the time he was a teenager in high school to find his way in the world, to fit in with other people like he saw others do easily and without effort, but was never successful. No matter what he tried, he found himself held objectionable by most of his fellow students, the teachers expressed no regard or encouragement for a career direction for him, it would have been an impossible task for an expert Personal Psychoanalyst to fit this young man in a career direction for talent, he seemed to have none.

    He had tried everything to fit into the world. He was in the National Guard for a year, worked on a pig farm, worked in a Quick Lube, worked as a mechanic, got fired from most of them for tardiness, absence or just incompetence. The only talent he ever demonstrated was the dubious distinction of having a reputation around Maximo of being able to drive fast and skillfully.

His constant rejection and wary attitude of suspicion from people he met, created a hostile, disagreeable Chill Leonard who found it difficult to get along with most people. The only person he ever seemed to be able to interact with in a civil way was Trig Lamont who was known around Maximo as a guy who was into things, who seemed to do well, which intrigued Chill but what was more important to Chill Leonard, Trig Lamont always greeted him like he was a regular guy, by saying hello, giving him a wave when driving by the pool hall. He thought the world of Trig Lamont and they became not close friends, but casual friends and when Trig had approached him six months ago, Chill felt Trig proved his friendship with an unbelievable opportunity. Chill Leonard leaped at the proposal from Trig Lamont to drive the getaway car for Trig and his gang on a job they were planning.

Chill Leonard thought about these things while he was digging. When he finished he sat on the ground where he buried the money, closed his eyes and thought about the things he would do with his share. Then he recalled how he fouled up big time when he drove to visit his cousin Abe who ran a gas station on Highway 12 about twenty-five miles from Maximo, on the way back he was so fired up with the expectancy of his cut of the money and excited he foolishly went too fast and now he was sitting in a Cairo jail cell for speeding with an expired license.

Lying in his lower bunk listening to the news, Nelson Rockefeller was elected governor of New York, Alaska becomes the 49th state of the US, the United States nuclear submarine passes underneath the polar ice cap, but Chill wasn't interested in the news at all, until it was announced that breaking news of the Bank One robbery a few days ago in Akron would be released shortly. An hour later on the six o'clock morning news, over his prison radio he heard additional details of the shootout between his gang and the police. The police were finally releasing previously held information. The Police Commissioner reported the stopping of the vehicle driven by Trig Lamont and from the general identification of the descriptions of bank robbers resulted in a request by the police for the three bank robbers to get out of the car. Realizing they were caught, Bittle Remington fired from the back seat wounding the policeman beckoning them out of the car. Trig Lamont rolled out of the open car door to the ground, fired twice, wounding a sergeant ten feet away standing near a squad car. The other two squad cars blocking the road contained one officer each, armed with twenty gauge pump shot guns. They sent several volleys at the robbers in return fire. Trig Lamont was killed by shotgun blasts from two officers barricaded behind a squad car. Bittle Remington sprayed bullets from a semi automatic Glock at police who returned fire from two sides from pistols and pump shotguns blasting Shalop Rhodes to the ground. He was spread-eagled on the pavement barely breathing and was rushed to Akron General Hospital in an ambulance under police guard, operated on, and sent to intensive care in critical condition.

 Chill Leonard was terrified. If the gang members had talked, or if Shalop Rhodes survives and talks he knew it was all over for him. He was already in jail so he knew he would be immediately arraigned and charged and it would be all over for him. He was aware every moment what great danger he was in. Every minute of his remaining days in the Cairo jail for a speeding ticket he was expecting to be accused of participating in the Akron Bank One robbery on June 7th.

Nine days later he was surprised to be released from the Cairo jail and relieved he wasn't connected to the Akron bank robbery. He drove home to Maximo, still not sure whether the authorities were onto him or not, or if they made connections between him and the rest of the gang, so in fear of getting arrested at any time he packed a few things, told his folks he had news of a job for him down in Massilon where he had worked as a mechanic and knew a few people. He felt the urgency to escape the vicinity of the robbery. The only person he thought who might help him was Sandra Lemming, a waitress at the Cozy Café in Massilon. He had seen her on and off when he lived and worked there for a year, besides he didn't know anyone else to hole up with for awhile and he meant to entice Sandra Lemming into leaving the country with him when he dug up the money. It wasn't like they had been just casual friends, they had even lived together for a few months. She told him repeatedly he was ok, but she also said he just didn't treat her as generously as he should or treat her good enough, and if and when he could do better give her a call. Now Chill was flush and Chill meant to do this, if Sandra only knew what he had now, he snickered, she would chase him around instead of him pursuing her.

Driving carefully within the speed limits and following all the road rules Chill Leonard reached Massilon and went right to the Cozy Café on Washington and Polk Streets. He parked his souped up Chevy about a half block away where he found a parking spot, froze when a police car hurried by with lights flashing. Chill still lived in fright that Shalop Rhodes might have regained consciousness and would give him up for a deal putting him on the wanted list. But he never heard anything and at least he was in Massilon and would have a chance to run. Besides, he didn't want to be with his folks if they came to arrest him and make them accessories, even though they weren't involved.

Entering the Cozy Café Chill saw no changes, the four booths, towards the back on the left side, long counter on the right the length of the restaurant with twelve stools, behind the counter was the serving window with Oddysius Petroupoulous, the owner, sticking an order out every few minutes to Sandra Lemming or Lill Sanchez, the other waitress. There were people in three of the booths, two eating and one group of three awaiting their orders. Five of the stools had customers on them, four were men, two in hard hats, one in a suit, one with a leather jacket on, and one girl dressed like an office girl with a high collared blouse, suit jacket, matching tan skirt, medium heels, and thick brown horn rimmed glasses.

Sandra Lemming and Chill Leonard, despite their on again off again romance, were ill suited to each other with numerous incompatible tendencies, but shared one overwhelming attraction that provided each mutual pleasure in their barren lives. They gratified each other physically, neither had much luck with anyone else. They had over the last few years broken up, but got back together several times as their needs seemed to demand. Sandra had been without any companionship for several weeks now. When she saw Chill walk in she was unusually well pleased he came in. "Why Chill Leonard, you old flirt, where you been? I thought a lot about you," she lied.

"Hi Sandra, oh, here and there. Got to thinking about ya and here I am," he lied. Their lack of veracity to each other was just another iffy aspect contributing to the fragility of their relationship. He beckoned her closer with his finger, leaned over the counter close to her ear, "Sandra, I've got something to tell you that you won't believe, but you'll sure love to hear it. I'll tell you tonight, if I can stay with you for a few days."

Sandra Lemming looked at Chill with skepticism, he never had much good news before. Despite her lack of confidence in his glowing description of the news he had for her, she didn't say yes or no. Sandra Lemming wanted to be nice to Chill. She had treated him rather rough last time she saw him, but she had a use and a need for him now, at least temporarily, but she still hadn't made a decision whether to let him stay with her or not. She put a cup of coffee down in front of him, put her elbows on the counter, smiled, "For my favorite customer," she said patronizingly stroking his ego.

Sandra Lemming was ten years older than Chill Leonard, a head taller, slender, without much appeal, but she was a virile woman who needed a man for her gratification and her needs were of the intensity that demanded attention. Chill Leonard filled these requirements in a minimal way. Basically she found Chill Leonard nothing but someone to exploit and use to her whimsical satisfaction, in every way she could. He merely convenienced her which gave her the forbearance to tolerate him.

They spoke again on her break, then after his sincere sounding enthusiasm she gave him her apartment key. The thing that convinced her to put him up was the roll of bills he took out to pay for his breakfast and the twenty dollar tip he left. Her reasoning was with that kind of money his insistence of a great deal gained credibility in her mind. The next three weeks, Chill Leonard lived with Sandra Lemming, he took her to night clubs, fine dining places, shows, plays, and every time she expressed appreciation, he'd say, "Sandy you ain't got any idea what's to come for you."

Sandra kissed Chill Leonard on the ear, then nibbled on it, then licked it. Chill Leonard was thrilled. Sandra never favored him like that before. "My, I think you're going to earn your share of the dough if you keep coming up with gimmicks like that," he gushed.

Sandra Lemming pursed her lips, in a baby falsetto voice she cooed, "Anything sweet papa wants, sweet papa gets."

Chill Leonard was getting his first hint at how money can make one's life a pleasure.

Chill Leonard worried about his folks. He reasoned if he were identified they could have trouble so he called them occasionally to see how they were faring and to see if the law had been snooping around.

"Hello Pa, it's me Chill. How's everything with you and Ma?" Chill made small talk knowing if anything had happened Dad would tell him.

"Oh, everything's all right I guess. Nothing new around here to tell ya except that big company that bought the Granger farm next to ours is using the farm for parking their machinery, material and equipment. "I swear Chill it looks like they got about ten Caterpillars, ten front loaders and back loaders, ten graders, a pulverizing machine, twenty heavy trucks, ten Caterpillars with big buckets, about six cranes, levelers, two giant cement mixers, five graders and a hell of lot more that I can't see. It kinda looks they're like a rental company or something, it's hard to tell what yet. All the local boys around here that can handle heavy equipment tried to apply for jobs, but they weren't takin' any applications or doin' any hiring, so they ain't building nothing I guess, just usin' it as a parkin' lot an like I said maybe they're in the rental business."

"Gee Pa, at least your house is a few miles from the property line, no noise will bother you and Ma no matter what they do there."

"I guess, Chill. When ya coming up home son?"

"Oh, by and by, you know I'm working down here you know," he lied. "When the job gives out I'll be back.

The Monday of the following week Chill again called his folks in Maximo. There was

Ten Stories of Mystery – Suspense – Adventure – Intrigue

no answer so he tried again the following day. This time his mother answered. "Hi Mom." Chill was concerned about his parents, but his latest excessive interest was to indirectly get an idea if the authorities had in any way showed up which would tell Chill they were on to him and give him time to flee.

"Chill, your dad went to the hospital two days ago. He got those chest pains again like he had last year. He'll be in there for a few days I guess. I go to the hospital every day. I hope he ain't in there too long, it's kinda strange being here without Pa."

Chill found out what he wanted to know, no one apparently was onto him. He gleefully envisioned what he would do with all the money, the life of luxury, the existence in a fantasy world he always dreamed of but never thought he would ever see.

"Sandra we can think about pulling up stakes here shortly. We'll swing up to visit my folks, take care of a few things up there, then paradise here we come baby," then he clapped and rubbed his hands together laughing.

When he called home the third week his mother told him his father had never left the hospital. After the tests this time they found one artery 70% blocked, one artery 85% blocked and they had wheeled him to surgery the second day he had entered the hospital three weeks earlier. She said the doctors said he might be able to go home within the week.

"So will he make a full recovery Ma?"

"Doctors say so, but they told him he can't do much of anything for about six months. You know your dad, this'll kill him."

"Well, he was lucky they caught it in time or he wouldn't have made it this far."

"That's what I tell him every day I visit him."

"Ma, I'll be home in a few days. I'll visit awhile to check on dad and then I'll be off on a good job down in Florida. It's such a good deal I can't turn it down."

"Well that's good son. I have to go now, Evaline is running me to the hospital. I'll be goin' now."

"Ok, love ya Ma." Chill heard the click of his mother's phone as she hung up.

Chill Leonard was in high spirits. No hint of any heat on him at all so he decided he was pretty much safe now. If Shalop Rhodes had regained consciousness and he hadn't given Chill up maybe he would get by this after all.

The first day of the fourth week Chill Leonard left Sandra's apartment and went to the Cozy Café for breakfast as usual. Sandra was already at work. He told Sandra that she should quit her job waitressing, they would be heading north for a few days. "When you quit, remember you'll never have to work tables again or at nothing else either."

She believed Chill Leonard because he had told her this over and over again, his comments had weight seeing he had plenty of money. He didn't leave any more twenty dollar tips, explaining to Sandra he couldn't afford to draw any attention to himself and then said one day he'd explain. He did, however, slip her money from time to time at home with such generosity, Sandra Lemming was convinced his story of good fortune was the truth. She commented several times Chill was finally treating her right.

As Chill Leonard was sipping his coffee and eating his breakfast, the TV in the back of the room, up in the corner near the ceiling of the Café, flashed the picture of

Police Commander Hodges of the Cairo Police Department giving an update on the Bank One Akron bank robbery. Chill froze with fright, terrified he would be part of the announcement. Commander Hodges announced that Shalop Rhodes, the last surviving bank robber, died of gun shots wounds in the Akron General Hospital at 1:45 that morning from fatal wounds received in the shoot out at the road block at 25th Street and Main. The money had not been recovered yet, but the search for the money would continue. Chill Leonard was both stunned and frightened, wondering if Shalop had regained consciousness long enough to have given the police his name as the fourth bank robber. But when he thought about it he thought if the police had his name they would have issued his picture and alerted the public that he was armed and dangerous. Chill was relieved, now that Shalop Rhodes was dead he hoped and prayed he was free and clear.

Suddenly it struck him that he was the only survivor of the robbery gang. He had all the money now, it was all his, instead of a one fourth split he now had it all. It was the first time in his life he had something really big go his way.

"What are you so happy about Chill? I never saw you wear a smile like that before."

"Never had this much to smile about before."

Despite being ten years older than Chill, that night Sandra Lemming again proved as frisky as a mare in heat, as horny as Chill was she exhausted him into total satiation, finally causing him to turn away from her in bed to rest. She always had the ability to do that, and he didn't mind a bit.

Chill convinced Sandra Lemming she would be able to quit her job with glowing promises of such magnitude of prosperity that she was infused with the same euphoria that Chill was experiencing and he swore repeatedly he would share with her. When she would ask, "Share what?" Chill would chuckle. "When the time's right you'll know," was all he'd say.

Chill Leonard had been gone from Maximo over four weeks now. Now that Shalop Rhodes was dead Chill felt completely relaxed for the first time since the robbery. There was no mention of him on the news, no mention of a fourth robber, no sign that anyone was looking for him, so he called his father to see if everything was ok with his parents. His dad said, "Son, it's right nice hearing from you. Ma and me is looking forward to seein' ya soon, but I gotta go now. Ma's waiting outside for me to take her to church."

Early Monday morning just as the horizon showed a rim of light before the sun peeked out, Chill and Sandra with gleeful anticipation headed out on Highway Nine headed north towards Maximo and the money. They drove an hour, stopped in for breakfast at a bus stop outside of Fulton, then with luxurious abandon spent two hours at a motel on the outskirts of Canal.

Leaving the motel the wind had gusted, dark black clouds had sped in overhead and the rain began lightly then increased to a steady, heavy downpour, clouding vision, wind buffeted the car swaying it at times. For better control and safety Chill reduced his speed from seventy miles an hour to fifty miles an hour. Cars were speeding by as Chill was heading north to Maximo. Two hundred yards in the opposite lane of oncoming traffic a sleek, gypsy red 1955 Corvette with a V8 engine generating 195 horsepower

Ten Stories of Mystery – Suspense – Adventure – Intrigue

had been passing cars weaving in and out. The Corvette passed a muddy GMC SUV, pulled in behind a silver semi truck spraying rain off his sides and from his back wheels misting the vision of the Corvette. The Corvette pulled out to pass, the rain caused the driver to misjudge the oncoming car, in hurrying to cut back into his lane in front of the silver semi-truck the high powered Corvette was nicked on the tip of his bumper by the semi-truck, sending it skittering sideways on the wet pavement, smashed into the guard rail, turned over and over tumbling into the culvert. The semi jack knifed, hitting Chill Leonard's souped up Chevy with the side of his cab, crushing the driver's side, killing Sandra Lemming instantly. Chill Leonard was taken unconscious to Canal Community Hospital with minor injuries, his luck due to the angle of impact with the semi truck and his seat belt.

A week later Chill was discharged from the hospital, bought a clean looking used car from a used car lot in Fulton from a cigar chomping fast talking Clyde Clodsle thinking if he bought a new car with cash it would bring unwanted attention to him. Chill resumed driving toward his home in Maximo, rueful and sorry about what happened to Sandra Lemming. With passing regret and sorrow he lamented Sandra would no longer be around, but then when he thought deeply about it he grimaced, thinking, oh well, with all my money I'll be able to have no trouble to replace her and sped on, eager to dig up his buried money.

This shallow regard for people escaped Chill Leonard, that one of the reasons he had no friends was he never learned to be one or to allow himself to be genuinely uninhibited in developing feelings for others.

Chill Leonard turned off the main highway at Fulton Ohio, took a right onto a two lane highway. As he rolled toward home, he thought of his unhappy school days with cringing memories of coolness and rejection by his classmates, his recollections included the teachers who indicated pretty clearly his prospects for success was slender. While he resented these negative incidents, he laughed to himself, with the comfort of knowing when he gets his hands on the buried money from the Bank One job he will have more than anyone that ever knew him. With this smug feeling he turned off on County Road J, a dirt road, turned north again, approaching the Leonard farm, turned into the long, winding driveway, drove up, swung past the flower bed that his mother prized, swung into the old hay barn now used only for a garage. He saw no cars in the garage, walked up to the house hoping to see his parents, intending to leave immediately with the buried money.

He walked in the kitchen door. The kitchen appeared unused since breakfast, no dishes on the table or in the sink, the towels hanging neatly arranged on racks across the sink. The cleanliness was the way Ma Leonard kept her home, she even insisted Pa, Evaline and Chill remove their shoes when they entered the house.

"Anybody here?" Chill called out. He walked to the foot of the stairs, yelling up loudly, "Anybody home?" Not getting an answer, Chill headed for the barn whistling Swanee River with a lilt to his voice and moving his head from side to side in cadence with the song, in jovial spirits with the anticipation of retrieving all his money. He went into the corner of the barn, grabbed a shovel and started walking through the woods to the fence line where beyond ten feet on the next property was where he buried the money. His excitement made him giddy. Growing more eager as he approached the edge of the Leonard farm, Chill passed through the few remaining trees on the northern border and viewed the abutting property where he had buried his money.

His mouth sagged as he gaped at what he saw, his feeling of sinking, whirling with total confusion, refusal to consider what he was seeing and refusing to acknowledge in his mind what he was witnessing, stunned and transfixed him in a stupor. Chill, with a dizzying sensation, sunk to his knees to better absorb the shock he was suffering. The once lush green sloping hill was gone. What Chill saw was only level land teeming with men and machinery, hundreds of men, wearing hard hats, tractors, scrapers, bull dozers, trucks moving back and forth some with loads of dirt, cement trucks loading cement at huge portable cement mixers, dozens of buildings, some with metal trusses supporting metal roofs, many huge round metal silo storage units, were already in the finishing stages, having ladders welded to the sides, metal doors installed, hundreds of carpenters, electricians, brick layers were busily plying their trades while the buildings were springing up as Chill watched. A prefabricated stone building stood over the burial site where he had hidden the money. In dismay, Chill simply watched the frantic activity and pace of the construction teams, realizing all was lost, but long after he finally accepted the fact he had lost his fortune, he still lingered, twelve feet from the fence line somehow dissipating his crushing disappointment by just being near where he had cached the money.

The thing that hurt the most was the fact that all the people from his young childhood, through school, his teachers, all proved their prophecies were correct. Chill Leonard was a loser.

Identity of a Coward

Capt McCoy was behind the desk signing up a young man, Toddy Ames, for a one year stint as a Texas Ranger. Toddy was still at the age where it was unnecessary to shave, but he was a sturdy looking lad. In the brief informal interview and test Capt. McCoy found he was an uncommonly fine shot, hitting center of the target six times. No other recruit ever did that before, in fact it was that performance that swayed Capt. McCoy to take the lad on, after all, shooting straight was what it was all about wasn't it? Todd Ames had been given the oath and shown a bunk. He brought his own horse, had his own rifle and Colt. Being so much younger Toddy didn't have much in common with the older men. They accepted Toddy, but not with alacrity, more like a tolerance. The men felt more assured with mature men to ride with which was a preference they felt but left unsaid.

A rider galloped through the stockade gate, skidded his dust covered lathered horse to a stop, ran into the small crude wood-sided building that was called Headquarters for C Troop of the Texas Rangers.

"Capt., Soldano's been raiding north of El Paso again. Hit the Eberheart and Corcoran Rancherios late last night, got most of the live stock, killed two. Capt. McCoy had pursued Soldano and his raiding, killing band of cutthroats for the better part of a year without success. Soldano's men were mounted on the finest horseflesh in the area, they rustled only the best. The two times Captain McCoy's troop had Soldano's gang in sight they couldn't catch them as they were better mounted than they were. The troopers' mounts were furnished by themselves, some of the their horses were anything but swift, some just all purpose former farm horses.

"Damn it," Capt. McCoy yelled out to Sgt. Holmes. "Tell Johnny to bugle the boys out, have the men ready to go with three days provisions."

Twenty-five miles from El Paso the Ranger column of seven men were ambushed by Mescalero Apaches. The fire fight lasted an hour and a half, one trooper dead, one wounded, one missing. An exhausted trooper by the name of Corporal Blodgett exclaimed, "That young Ames must have taken off like a blaze when the shootin' started."

Corporal Weems, a stocky young man, a two year veteran was bandaging his left arm that was scraped open by an Apache arrow. "Well, it's better we found out now instead of later when he could a got some more of us killed, when we were really depending on him."

Someone said, "Well some fight, some run."

Another voice chimed in, "A coward's a coward I guess, no matter what. Some don't have what it takes."

The troopers in C Company never talked about Toddy Ames again, never mentioned the cowardice of Toddy Ames, they all had such pride in the troop and the deeds they performed they erased the event from their memory.

The troop began setting up camp for the night. They got the hobbles from the saddle horns, tended to their horses then scattered around the fire. Taking time to lick their wounds, the men were thankful for the rest.

One man was cleaning his rifle and Colt, one was sewing his torn vest, one was etching his name on his badge with the tip of his knife.

The following nine months a funny thing happened. No news and no atrocities by Cordiero Soldano's wicked band were reported, it was like the earth opened up and they were swallowed up. "Sure is strange Captain. The way Soldano disappeared ain't it?"

The captain looked at Corporal Blodgett, "I didn't know you liked him so much to miss him."

"I didn't say I liked him and I didn't mean I miss him, I just meant I ain't heard about him in awhile."

"Well then say what you mean, will ya?"

A year after the Apache engagement, twenty-five miles from El Paso the troop now eleven strong, had traveled south and west of El Paso where they were familiar with the area having chased Soldano's band around there so many times They even identified a former campsite they had once occupied. "Hey Captain, over here, see this!" he shouted a discovery of sorts in his voice.

The troop descended into the huge hog wallow reading the signs of a tell tale struggle. There were three skeletons off to one side, partially covered by drifting sand, a black tip of a black cord was visible. Trooper Larson pulled on it and a partially buried hat that was gold trimmed, corded with gold braid, decorated with tassels, was pulled out. "The trade mark and calling card of Soldano. Why we ain't heard of ol' Soldano cause he's been killed right here." There were three other skeletons scattered about who were in the fight too, two of the skulls had bullet holes that were dead center between the eyes.

"Wow," trooper Higgins said, "that man could sure shoot, one between the eyes could be lucky, two is skill the way I see it."

Twenty-five feet over the rim of the wallow behind a cactus was another skeleton and a bullet hole above the right eye. "Holy hell that bunch picked on the wrong hombre, but it looks like they got him though. Well, let's see what his skeleton can tell us." The two men examined the skeleton, found no broken bones, no chipped bones. "Captain what do you think happened?"

"Well I figure he got 'em all, was wounded, and no help around, bled to death. The troopers agreed it probably happened that way because the weapons lay rusted where they fell which meant everyone in the shootout was killed. Here and there around the battle scene they found a rusting Colt, a few rusted Winchesters, by the far corpse that Capt. McCoy wondered who the unlucky cowboy that was jumped by Soldano's band was, no one was reported missing or unaccounted for in the last nine months.

Trooper Anthony McIntyre found a piece of metal covered with patina crusted around. He took his bowie knife and scraped it off revealing the shape of a star. "Why this may have been a sheriff or some kind of law man." The trooper took sand, wet a rag, began buffing the star and after about fifteen minutes of harsh rubbing the trooper looked closely at the buffed star. Trooper McIntyre examined the star, squinted his eyes, "Captain, Captain, look at this."

Captain McCoy took the star. "Well I'll be darned." The inscription read, Tod Ames.

The boys all suffered from having used expletives when referring to Toddy Ames's disappearance. He must have gotten separated in the Apache fire fight, stayed low, got clear then was jumped by Soldano's band much to their misfortune. The sharpshooting lad took them all out. The remorse felt by each man was immeasurable, but they said what they said, so their shame and embarrassment was earned, but their admiration and respect for the lad was of monumental dimensions. The greatest topic of conversation in C Troop now was the legendary feat of Toddy Ames, the lad who wiped out Cordiero Soldano's wicked, murderous band single handedly in the greatest feat a C Trooper ever performed.

The Improvident

When someone requested all fools to rise, everyone in the room would rise if their tendency to avoid embarrassment could be subdued. I personally pled guilty to having been every kind of fool but a few. I had squandered my patrimony, made a disastrous selection in matrimony, conjured up more than my share of acrimony with my faulty judgments with women. You foolishly repeat your follies.

Despite my dissatisfaction and failure with Ida Kaloon in matrimony, the afternoon I espied Mona Reilly I was hers. She was a few days shy of eighteen, with skin like white cream, a short thin nose with delicate nostrils, full inviting lips, with pale reddish hair, possessing beautiful solemnity with the grace of rhythmic movement coupled with a naivety of innocence that I didn't intend to alter the unawareness of in her.

Mona's father was a preoccupied man hiding behind a full beard from ear to ear around his mouth and chin, oblivious to everything around him unless it crawled, flew, and was a member of the insect world. He squinted through his wire spectacles mounting specimen after specimen only acknowledging his daughter Mona because she provided him food, looked after his clothes, kept his alcohol bottles for preserving specimens full, and a supply of whiskey that he claimed sharpened his abilities to do superior mountings of insects due to the inspiration he seemed to receive from the relaxed state it put him in.

My irritation was aroused when another besides myself coveted the interests of Mona Reilly. It was Cordell Ames, a recent arrival from college, having the advantage of being exposed to Latin, Greek, Italian, algebra, calculus, plus advanced geometry. The man was truly a formidable adversary, as I was enveloped in playing baseball, a movie now and then, pool, brick laying and pleasant female company. With these incompatibilities you would hardly think we could even become casual friends, but as our common goal was Mona Reilly we became wary confederates in cause. In the subtle masked insincere conversations steeped with verisimilitudinous deception of camaraderie we continually tried to gauge who was winning the race. Even when the three of us conversed neither Cordell nor I could detect the direction Mona Rielly was leaning. What Cordell and I discovered was that Mona was adept since the cradle at keeping people from guessing what she was about at any time.

As absent minded as professor Reilly was he perceived through his obtuseness where his daughter was concerned that there was a threat to the use of this person who provided him with food and took care of his clothes from the presence of these two young men who were trying to cast a butterfly net over her to acquire their own specimen. With undisguised prejudice the professor assigned Cordell and I in the roll of impediments to his work and banned us from the premises, assigning both as to being inferior to specimens in his entomology pursuits.

Cordell and I stayed away for ten days to allow the man's wrath to subside. When we returned in duo we found the house vacant, closed, they were gone without a word or clue. We agreed to collaborate and track the runaways down. We checked the ticket agent at the bus terminal, the railroad station and the airlines meeting with total failure to get even a hint of where the runaways were. From the joint effort Cordell and I became casual, insincere friends but worse enemies. Cordell had a demeaning condescending way of prancing learning and belittling me, reducing me to the image of, "See Spot Run, Dick and Jane."

We nevertheless met after work several times a week to find out from each other if anything of the Reilly's was learned. We played chess and tried to work up new ideas of what to attempt. One afternoon Cordell Ames said, "Suppose you did find her Tom? Mona has a mind, an appreciation for poetry, culture, with great potential for growth. What can you offer her? I have found no one who enjoyed these things more than Mona. Don't you think you are wasting your time seeking her out?"

"Ames, you're knowledgeable about a lot of things, but not women."

Abilene's commercial establishments ignored the Sabbath, they didn't want to

Ten Stories of Mystery – Suspense – Adventure – Intrigue

forego one seventh of a week's profit. Saturday nights were big and big profits. Tom preferred the Alhambra on the corner of Cedar and Grant. It was one of the more opulent gambling halls in Abilene. The bar was solid mahogany, sixty feet long, the fittings all brass, an array of nude paintings positioned strategically so there was no unfavorable vantage point no matter where a patron sat. Tom spotted someone getting up from a table of five and he walked over.

"Welcome," the dealer said. The rest of men just glanced, most gave Tom an impersonal nod. "Seven card stud boys," the dealer announced.

The cigar chewing whiskey drummer opened, three of the four players raised with optimism and expectations for their hands. The betting continued with spirit until the last card was to be turned up, even the last hand saw several different players raise the bet thinking their hand was superior, Tom wondered if he read his cards wrong, he had four of a kind, usually a formidable hand in poker. The last hand saw two more raises, the man in mining clothes was fifty dollars short. According to the rules of table stakes if you can't cover the bet you are out of the game. "Boys," he said, "I'm short fifty dollars, but everybody willin' I'll put up a gold claim that I was offered up to five thousand dollars for, if I had the assay report you'd see what I mean." The players shrugged, smirked, nodded ok. The last card came down and Tom won a pile of cash and a signed deed to a gold claim.

The next afternoon when he met with Cordell Ames at the "Water Hole Saloon," neither man had anything new on the whereabouts of Mona Reilly. They lamented, exchanged superlatives of their mutual missing beauty. "Cordell, maybe we could hire a detective agency to find the professor and Mona?"

"Hey do you realize how much that would cost? Neither one of us could afford it."

Tom took the deed to his gold mine out of his pocket, pushed in front of Cordell Ames and told him about his luck at the Alhambra. "This can get us the money we need Cordell. If you put up half the money we'll find the mine, get it working, split what dust we get and pay for a detective to find Mona."

"I don't know," Cordell said, "the whole scheme sounds risky and we don't even know if the mine exists."

"Look," Tom Saddler said, "there are specific landmarks each step of the way. There's no mystery here. What could be easier?"

Cordell Ames thought about his longing to see Mona Reilly and rolled over in his mind how he may never have that chance unless he did something extraordinary. "Ok Tom, I'm skeptical, but I'll partner with you on this, not because I think it's sensible, only because it looks like our only choice."

"You might feel better Cordell with the fact the old prospector told me the mine had an assay stamp on it from Dodge City which was high, and it's down track from Larned not to far. Check it out if it'll make you feel better."

This seemed to temporarily neutralize Cordell Ames's cynicism. By the time they detrained at Larned, Cordell seemed more comfortable with their project. At the livery on Prairie Avenue, Tom and Cordell purchased two horses, a mule, shovels, pick, pan, miners pick hammer, saw and hammer to make a sluice, then cooking utensils, coffee pot, skillet, a slab of bacon, and coffee. The burro was so loaded the remaining few items they needed they stored behind the cantles of their saddles. At the hotel they each paid half the bill, continuing to honor their agreement of sharing expenses.

They decided to dine in the hotel before they headed out. They feasted on thick juicy steaks, roasted potatoes, ears of corn, and peach pie. "This may be the last feast and the biggest we'll have for awhile after we hit the trail and have to eat our own cookin'," said Tom.

"Whew, that was some feed alright," exclaimed Cordell Ames, then paused in remembrance, "but I was just thinking little Mona Reilly could have handled it easier than we did. That little beauty could sure pack it in."

Tom laughed, "Well, if that's what it takes to get that beautiful I'm for women eating a lot."

Following the detailed instructions on the back of the deed to the mine, they found what looked like two stone obelisks fashioned by nature anomalously but not mistakenly. Overjoyed, they read the next instruction to locate an oak tree in the midst of a copse of pine trees which would point them to the mine. Tom and Ames were jubilant, they could hardly control their excitement, then their enthusiasm began to waver. They couldn't find the oak tree, and worse than that, there was no copse of pines.

"I should of known better," moaned Cordell Ames. "I can't believe I allowed myself to be taken in like this. This was a bilk from the start you boob."

A dejected Tom Saddler said, "We can look for the mine, can't we? It'll just take longer."

"Are you a slow learner Saddler? You've been swindled and you're too dense to see it. I can't believe I got into such a ridiculous venture." They both turned towards a speck of dust starting to rise into a rooster tail from the Holiday stage heading to Larned. "Saddler, this idiotic scheme of nonsense is all yours. I'm heading back. I'm sorry I ever met you, you're a fool." Cordell Ames intercepted the stage, boarded and headed back home to Abilene leaving Tom with his folly.

Tom Saddler for the next three years lived with his vision and dream of Mona Reilly never having given up seeking her.

Tom saddler had sent letters of inquiry everywhere there was a possibility they might have heard of a professor Reilly, to no avail. Tom Saddler moved from Abilene, Kansas to Cheyenne Wells, Colorado, a small town 120 miles southeast of Denver. There was no newspaper in Cheyenne Wells, but Burlington, a town north of Cheyenne Wells had one and Tom read a small notice that the Entomological Society was holding their annual meeting in the Radison Hotel in Denver on the 10th of next month. It was the first time it was held west of St. Louis. Tom had written to them several times in the past for news of Professor Reilly with total failure. Tom Saddler felt no optimism this time either, but his commitment forced him to try. A letter to the Society in Denver produced no results. Tom Saddler had never gone to an Entomological convention, but he determined he would investigate it on a chance that someone might have known Professor Reilly.

When Tom Saddler arrived at the Radison Hotel on the 10th of the month, he found at the reception desk to his disappointment, there was no Professor Reilly on the list of attendees. Despite not being assigned a place setting at a table in the banquet room, Tom went into the crowded dining room as people were gradually finding their assigned dinner places, inquiring from one person after another if they had any knowledge of a Professor Reilly from Wichita Community College. He had interrogated seven tables and at one table five of the members had found their places. "Pardon the intrusion gentlemen," Tom Saddler inquired, "would any one of you have any knowledge of a professor Albion Reilly? He is an entomologist, but he is not on the roster of attendees..." One of the gentlemen interrupted, "Sir, it's true he is not listed, but he is here. I have seen him.

A white whiskered balding gentlemen in a rumpled suit with a traditional professorial look of careless sartorial standards replied, "We might not, but I believe there is a Professor Boslowitz that coauthored a research paper with Reilly a few years ago. He is here somewhere and he possibly can be of assistance to you."

Tom Saddler dashed with expectations to the reception desk where he obtained the name, table number and seat of Professor Boslowitz and then threaded his way back through the dense milling crowd to table fifty-four. The table was full. Professor Boslowitz said in response to Tom Saddler's inquiry, "Yes sir," and waved a hand at a man in a dark blue suit, a string tie, long flowing grey hair reaching to his shoulders, a full beard from his upper lip, up to his ears, covering his chin. Full recognition flashed into Tom Saddler's mind, he had found Professor Reilly.

Professor Reilly leaped up, "Why Tom, young man, how nice to see you after all this time. Come, we must talk and catch up."

Chairs were spread and room made for Tom to his utter amazement. Tom was shocked at the warmness and friendliness of Professor Reilly's greeting. His recollections of being banished from his premises, his coldness, aloofness and yes his hostility was fixated in his mind. He was wondering if an inquiry about his daughter Mona would rekindle his former hostility, but she was the reason for this quest wasn't she? "Professor, may I inquire of Mona's well being sir?"

"You may indeed young man, you may indeed. She would have been distressed if you made no inquiries of her."

"That is a comfort to hear sir. Perhaps she would enjoy a visit from an old friend?"

"Why my boy she would be most disappointed if you neglected to give her the pleasure."

Tom Saddler never felt so good since the first time he espied Mona Reilly. Tom Saddler was confused by the drastic change in the preferences of Professor Reilly. Tom hadn't accomplished much since he saw Mona and her father, they could tell he wasn't a roaring success, he hadn't acquired wealth, it certainly wasn't his charm and charisma. What was it then? Well, Tom Saddling didn't care. His driven mission to find the one girl that was the key to his happiness for the rest of his life was now in reach. Tom sent a succession of pictures across his imagination, a wife, children, an orchard with sublime eternal happiness for the rest of his life with the woman he had long cherished.

Tom was expected in two weeks by Mona and Professor Reilly in their home in Tulia, Texas, a small town eighty miles from

Amarillo. Tom spent most of his money on a new corduroy jacket, new Levi's, a tall brimmed white hat with a rattlesnake band, a new double pocket shirt with pearl buttons, and new hand tooled boots. He meant to advance his new found acceptance with a dazzling sartorial display of elegance. The train ride though bumpy, sooty, jarring and jerky was somehow not only not unpleasant to Tom, but each bump and jolt represented nearing the elusive sought after one most dear to his life.

As my moment to enter paradise neared my knees felt weak. The road from Tulia turned into the most magnificent glorious valley I had ever seen. The valley was lush and green, with a cool refreshing stream winding through it. I had never seen so many birds, swarms of a multitudinous variety of butterflies of the diverse colors, even some I was seeing for the first time. Perhaps the touch of Professor Reilly was asserting his entomological magic for material for new specimens and a new scientific paper. It was then I heard the lilting voice of Mona softly singing a lullaby while she was gathering flowers. Mona Reilly stood up and again I saw the creamy white perfection of her flawless skin. I was shocked at the rest of her. It's not a far leap from the subtleties of illusion Tom Saddler had etched in his mind of Mona Reilly to the disturbing hallucination he thought he was experiencing now.

Mona Reilly said, "I'm so pleased you've finally found me Tom, it took you so long."

Mona Reilly was unchanged in her lovely oral vibrant tones, her voice was still the same melodious enchanting quality, clear, a cadence that gave her speech interest, singularity that attached uniqueness and thus pleasantry to anyone listening to her. But the sameness ended there. The vision of her now shattering the daily and nightly dreams fixated in my mind for years. He conceded to himself that all these years he was clinging to a nonexistent illusion. Now as I surveyed Mona with circumspection I found it incredulous, her arms were the size of shank hams, her legs were loose fleshed and flabby, now instead of shapely slender legs that were once firm, straight delightfully symmetrical, were now the size of small tree stumps. Her body was now overflowing with an excess of avoirdupois. He remembered how she had stunned

Cordell Ames and himself with her enormous consumption of food each time they had dined with her. Her condition was the result of her enormous capacity and gourmand treatment of all food in sight.

Professor Reilly, Mona and I dined at supper together. Mona ran true to form, out eating Professor Reilly and myself by at least three to one. I remembered in the café when I first saw this girl in the bloom of pulchritude how I yearned and prayed I would someday taste her romantic gifts. Now, as I observed the dear victim of excesses, any thought a romantic interlude with her was dismissed with repugnance. We enjoyed after dinner aperitifs, chatted quite a while. I fended off all overtures of offers of extended hospitality. I knew Mona and her father hinted at that I fit comfortably into the equation here increasing my alarm believing a rapid escape from here was now strategically required. The regal treatment they accorded me was sincere, but I was not too dense to detect the real objective was to clap a butterfly net over me and add me to the Professor's specimen boards. I courteously rejected an invitation to stay a few weeks, it would have been too painful to look at the mountainous load of fat that my dream girl had expanded into, and I knew I could not keep up my pretense that I didn't notice her bountiful physical condition and continue to refrain from commenting on the spectacle.

I pleaded the necessity to return to my job or I would lose it. I shook Professor Reilly's hand goodbye, pecked Mona Reilly's flabby cheek lightly, felt relieved when I was out of their sight. The entire reunion had taken on a spiritless conventionality. I sat at the train station staring at nothing, too stunned to digest all that I saw when I after years finally had found Mona Reilly, which conjured up feelings of regret, now knowing if I didn't find her I could have enjoyed the memory of the vision, the desire and the expectation of never having the image of Mona Reilly taken from me. I would have given anything not to have found Mona Reilly.

Cryptic Suicide

One morning after a delightful breakfast with her loving husband, then spending a pleasant hour going over the household agenda with the Cockney maid Brenda Covington, directly after receiving two gentlemen visitors one after the other, Bette Wellington sauntered up the shiny long mahogany staircase, went into the master bedroom, removed her husband's Magnum 57 from their bedside table drawer, and inserted one shell. She had a fixed stare like she was in another place and another time. She slowly raised the pistol to her head and shot herself. Nellie the cook in the kitchen jerked her head hearing the reverberation. The gardener Bill Schiller rushed through the kitchen door with shears still in his hands, excitedly looking around. "Nellie, was that a shot I heard?"

"Lord, I don't know!" she said, running to the bottom of the long winding oaken staircase. "Mrs. Wellington! Mrs. Wellington!" she shouted. "Are you alright? Bill, there's no answer, let's take a look. It doesn't look right."

They hurried up the long winding staircase, walked hurriedly to the end of the hall. There they saw Mrs. Bette Dexter Wellington lying in her own pool of blood, dead. Nellie, nervous in grief bit her finger, "Oh my God," she croaked. She called the police, the corporate office of Jon Wellington's company, Precision Instruments, left word his wife was in a tragic accident and he should come home immediately.

The family doctor was the one to inform Jon Wellington of his wife's death. It was painful and difficult for Dr. Morgan as he was the family doctor ministering to Bette and Jon Wellington for their entire married life. Dr. Morgan had never seen a happier married couple. They lacked children but were still both hopeful. Bette Wellington was normal, healthy, with a cheerful rosy optimism and a pleasing disposition. Everyone thought Jon Wellington a very lucky man for having such a pleasing, pleasant, agreeable wife.

Jon Wellington was a broken man. He had aged perceptively in just the few hours since he had spoken with Dr. Morgan and the police. Jon Wellington was perplexed with his mind in disarray. After the police determined that the tragic death took place between ten to twelve o'clock, he kept asking himself over and over again what could have happened after the time he left her at breakfast to cause his wonderful wife to do away with herself. Holding his drooping head between his hands, he repeated several times, "How could she have taken her own life? We were so happy, we loved each other, there was no reason for her to do this, no reason at all. Why just last night she was all excited about the trip we were planning to visit Germany, Switzerland, Austria and Luxemburg." Jon Wellington was impatient, irked, besieged not only by the loss of his dear wife but no one had any idea what happened. Neither Dr. Gorden nor the police said much except that the investigation would be vigorously pursued.

A few days later the official inquest labeled the death a suicide, much to the disbelief of Jon Wellington. He and his beloved wife of four years were happily married, there was no reason for her to take her own life and he meant to find out what happened. He called his director of security of his companies, Pete Hamil, a retired FBI district chief, and issued instructions to find the best investigator available. Emil Dodds in San Francisco was reputedly a tenacious, meticulous man with the instincts of a blood hound who produced results. He had solved jewel heists, insurance fraud schemes, even a kidnapping. He was the most able man available to hire. "Get him Pete, no matter the cost. I want to find out what happened to my wife. We were so happy I don't believe it was suicide at all."

Mr. Dodds was an unimpressive appearing man. He was five foot seven inches tall, wore glasses, had a fringe of hair from ear to ear, shiny bald on top, hardly the appearance of a an outstanding investigator, but his scholarly appearance seemed to encourage people to be inclined to talk freely with him. Mr. Dodds conferred with Detective Marino at the Effingham Police Department's 25th District Homicide Department for several hours, getting all of the available information on the case.

Beginning the following day Mr. Dodds began his work by interviewing Nellie the cook, Brenda Covington the English maid, Bill Schiller the gardener, and Alfred Eames the butler. They all confirmed Bette Wellington had two men callers, between ten and twelve o'clock that morning. The Effingham police department had already began efforts to locate and bring the men in for questioning, even though Mrs. Wellington was alive and well when each of the men left. Dodds's mind flashed the possibility Bette Wellington was in pregnancy with a child with a lover, but this theory was completely discredited by the testimony of the domestic help. They each declared how devoted Bette and Jon Wellington were to each other and of their continuous daily demonstrations of complete attachment to each other. The close friends of the Wellington's who frequently socialized with them in card games, barbecues, the opera, basketball games, all attested to the complete filial devotion Bette and Jon exhibited towards each other at all times. They were free of any financial worries, and the thorough, shrewd Mr. Dodds could find no evidence of marital misbehavior on the part of Jon Wellington.

    Mr. Dodds was momentarily at a dead end, but he knew from long experience he could work around it. Mr. Dodds was now convinced that Bette Wellington's actions were not the result of anything Jon Wellington did. Mr. Dodds felt comfortable with this conclusion, he could never represent a murderer. Mr. Dodds said, "You know sir, I have poured over every letter, checked every address in your wife's personal pages, finding nothing that would give us an idea of her mind set prior to the tragedy. Now sir, you told me that you met your wife in France when you were visiting your friend Montiel Monserat at the wine festival In Champagne, is that correct?"

    "Yes, but I accidentally met my wife, I was never introduced to her formally. She bumped into me when turning away from an exhibition table."

    "Oh? You don't believe it was contrived out of opportunism to meet you then?"

    "Heavens no, I was the only seeker. She made no overtures toward me, not once, it was all my effort and then we fell in love and were married."

"You mentioned she was living with a relative who had adopted her when you met her?"

"Yes, her Auntie Kinkaid."

"Her guardian raised no protest or objection?"

"No, in fact she was quite pleased. She was grateful to me for volunteering to provide the expense to cover the cost of a person to attend her, replacing Bette you know. I thought it was the least I could do for her knowing she used mostly her own money to raise my wife from a little girl."

"The auntie then was not asked to accompany you to Effingham, Illinois?"

"On the contrary, she was asked to several times. You see, Bette was very fond of her aunt but the old woman declined, citing familiarity with Bordeaux, pleading all her friends were there and the climate suited her health and infirmities that discouraged her from travel."

"I see. Were the two ladies living in modest comfort when you first met them in Bordeaux?"

"They were housed pleasantly in a small villa living a quiet life. Bette fussed and fawned over the old lady with such gentility, tenderness and consideration that I was impressed with her capacity for kindness which is one of the things that endeared her to me."

"I take it your wife was limited in a social life with her preoccupation with her aunt?"

"Yes and it seemed since she was very young that she forfeited her own social life to tend her Aunt Kinkaid. What impressed me most was she didn't seem to mind the sacrifice, she seemed to enjoy total contentment at all times. She was a remarkable woman."

"What was her age when you married her?"

"Thirty-one."

"Was she ever married before, ever have a serious relationship?"

"No, none that she mentioned. Used to tell her I saved her from being an old maid. She said, "Perhaps it's that I never met anyone until you that turned my heart." Her aunt Kinkaid was present when she said it and said, "Jon, you have no idea how unaffected and free from womanly artifices Bette is, you are a very fortunate man," and I sure was."

Mr. Dodds felt obligated to ask, "Are you sure you want me to continue with this investigation sir? So far we have uncovered little of consequence and no clues. To gain a foothold on this we will have to dig into your wife's past, even explore her childhood, it may or may not produce results, but it will surely produce huge expense for you sir."

"Mr. Dodds, I am convinced that there is a hidden reason why this happened, that is the reason I hired you sir. I must have closure here."

"All right sir, if you're determined I'll proceed."

"What is your next strategy?"

"Flying to Champagne, France in the morning."

Mr. Dodds was greeted at Aunt Kinkaid's villa in the Chalet Dubois complex by a crisp plain looking woman, Charlene Katz, who was hired to attend Aunt Kinkaid when Bette left for Effingham, Illinois as a married woman. Mr. Dodds smiled, presented his card which Miss Katz used to announce Mr. Dodds's arrival.

A voice drifted to the door from the balcony, "Oh Mr. Dodds, please come on in. Wellington called to announce your visit."

Mr. Dodds stepped into an inner room, emerged out on a balcony exposing a stunning view of the local wine region. He introduced himself to Auntie Kinkaid who addressed Miss Katz, "Mr. Dodds will be asking me some sensitive personal questions, I would prefer he have complete privacy, you may have the afternoon off."

Mr. Dodds was surprised, his first investigative instinct prompted the thought Auntie Kinkaid wanted no one present. What would she be concerned about he wondered if that was the case. Auntie Kinkaid had thin, snow white hair, brown eyes, wore bifocals, was constantly bothered by an intermittent but persistent cough. "Have you found out about the poor dear's tragedy yet?"

"I regretfully have to say no. The reason I'm here is to see what help you can give us. Mr. Wellington felt you probably have greater knowledge of his wife than even he has."

Auntie Kinkaid looked pleased at the compliment, raised an eyebrow, "I spoke to

Jon, wrote to him expressing my deepest sorrow at Bette's tragedy."

"Did you correspond with your niece often?"

"Oh yes, almost every week. I have all her letters, you may have them if you wish. Her letters overflow with her expressions of love for Jon, her one disappointment was I wouldn't travel to see her, but as you see my condition won't allow me the pleasure. I loved Bette deeply and do miss her so, but her happiness came first you know.

"Mr. Wellington informed me he provided you with funds to provide you with help to take the place of Bette."

"Oh my, no one could take the place of Bette. At my age I was irritable at times, difficult at times, sometimes even fractious and Bette never lost her patience or her equanimity, she was such a sweet kind person. Miss Katz does good work but there was only one Sweet Bette." She sniffled and dabbed her eyes with a laced handkerchief.

Mr. Dodds was always a bit hesitant and leery about someone who seemed a perfectly unselfish altruistic person and he got the feeling that this woman was trying hard to adopt that image. "Well, did Bette and Mr.

Wellington see to your situation to your satisfaction now that she was leaving you?"

"Yes, my niece insisted I contact her if I ever need anything, as I said, Jon Wellington gave me an allowance to acquire domestic help. Will it continue do you know?"

"I'm afraid I have no knowledge of that."

Mr. Dodds detected a tinge of avidity mentioning allowances in lieu of an expected plethora of questions of her niece's last few days and hours before her death and the circumstances on that fateful morning. This interesting contradiction resolved Mr. Dodds to take a closer look at Auntie Kinkaid. "While Bette was with you was there anything in her past that might have had an influence in her suicide?"

"What on earth do you mean?"

"Oh, like a disappointed love, a broken engagement, a jealous suitor?"

"Oh no, Jon was the only love in her life. She never sought out people her own age, never seemed to want to, she was self contained and quite composed."

"Was she active in school at all?"

"I home taught her when she was small, when she was older she was a home body."

"Could I see some photos of Bette when she was small?"

"Well actually I never was a camera buff and never had a camera then, but I do have an album somewhere. Would you like to see it?"

"It's probably a good idea." Mr. Dodds noticed Auntie Kinkaid bolt out of her wheelchair and scoot into the bedroom, raising a question about her comment she was too much of an invalid to travel to see Bette.

Mr. Dodds paged through dozens of pictures of Bette alone, with Auntie Kinkaid, in groups of people, of them at the Champagne Zoo, some when they had visited Paris, they even had a picture of them at the restaurant atop the Eiffel Tower.

Mr. Dodds was bothered there was not a single picture in the album when Bette would have been younger. "I know when I asked you if you had any snaps of Bette when she was around five or so you said no, but I forgot to ask if you had any professionally taken portraits of her at that age?"

"You know I feel so negligent, I didn't and I know there's no defense for it but I didn't."

Ten Stories of Mystery – Suspense – Adventure – Intrigue

"No matter. You came to Champagne when Bette was almost thirteen, but you adopted her when she was six, is that right?"

"Yes," Auntie Kinkaid croaked in an unsteady voice sensing she was getting into some intricacies she maybe couldn't extricate herself out of.

Mr. Dodds scented deception, omissions and untruthfulness intending to expose Auntie Kinkaid. "I understand Bette's father was your only sibling?"

"Yes, the only brother I had."

Mr. Dodds with his well trained ear to detect false statements was aware for awhile that Auntie Kinkaid was hiding something. Her voice flickered again suggesting a falsehood when she mentioned, "Only brother."

"What influenced you to adopt Bette at all?"

"Well, Mr. Dodd, her mother was dead, it was my duty. When my brother appealed to me he grieved about his fear of not being unable able to care for her properly saying he thought I was more capable of tending to her needs. What choice did I have really?" Auntie Kinkaid sighed, adopted a sweet pious benevolent, look, she fluttered her eye lashes histrionically, said in a cooing voice, "It was a duty of love you know."

"Did your brother provide financial assistance for the child's upkeep, education, other needs?"

"Yes he did, yes he did, but it wasn't sufficient, but if he wouldn't have done that I really would have been in difficulty. I willingly used my own money and we got by on my frugal management." Auntie Kinkaid again revealed a deceptive tendency to mingle facts and reasons, she leaned straight back in her wheelchair, appearing slightly miffed. "Now what can an allowance from my brother be of any possible interest to you or to Jon Wellington may I ask?"

Mr. Dodds was pleased that he found out Auntie Kinkaid was quite sensitive and defensive when finances were mentioned. Her demeanor changed from confidant sure answers to tentative faltering answers with full knowledge that her credibility and integrity was seeping into question if she wasn't careful.

"If Jon Wellington thought I had been careless with Bette's money all those years he should have asked me. I didn't do anything illegal, I just never told anyone about it. In fact there was no one to tell, but I guess I should have told Bette."

"Yes, you certainly should have done that all along." With Auntie Kinkaid's confused set of ethics Mr. Dodds didn't feel mentioning to her that maybe if she would have told Bette the loving, affectionate care Bette accorded her may not been quite so freely given and maybe she would not have been so willing to remain at home tending to Auntie Kinkaid so unselfishly.

"Mr. Dodd," Auntie Kinkaid said, "do you know if Mr. Wellington will be angered about how this looks and become vindictive?"

"I don't know why he would be or not, but he has every right to be angered by it."

"I know, I know," sniffled auntie Kinkaid, "but the majority of the money was properly spent on Bette so where is the illegality?"

"In failing to inform Bette, in not consulting her on the expenditures, the legal term I believe is called embezzlement in its harshest interpretation."

"Oh, my," Auntie Kinkaid sobbed anew at the reference to embezzlement. She wept, dabbed her eyes with a white handkerchief.

"Bette's father died in Norway five years later, the bank just kept sending the checks after they notified me of her father's death and with no other interested party I just let things continue the same way and kept spending her money."

Auntie Kinkaid left Dodds with the impression up to now that the allowance was too inadequate to supply Bette's needs. "Were you and your brother very close?"

Auntie Kinkaid's face took on a grim, defeated expression with a bewildering look of embarrassment. She knew to answer that question would be committing perjury and she feared the consequences of doing that. "Oh, Mr. Dodds," she whined, "I never met Bette's father."

Mr. Dodds in his long career had seen many extraordinary things that hardly affected him but when he heard what Auntie Kinkaid said, Mr. Dodds was so stunned, his eyebrows shot way up bugging his eyes out with his mouth agape from what he heard.

The old lady sniffled a few times more, then resumed, "I answered an ad in a London paper with a description of a position that may include an eventual adoption, with hints of quite proper remuneration which I was sorely in need of. I forwarded my qualifications through the Dublin Post, met with a lawyer in a London office, contacted three weeks later by the father who interviewed me but only on the phone, never met the man face to face. My business from that point on was with the attorney and the bank. I'm originally from Dublin you know, so the father was generous paying transportation fares back and forth to attend all the business I had to appear for."

Mr. Dodds was thinking that comparing Auntie Kinkaid to the father of Bette was like comparing two evil hardened, disgusting people. One abandoned and neglected a tot in need of love, guidance and direction; the other stole the child's money, misrepresented her role, creating in the child a nonexistent feeling of obligation to her as a benefactor when she actually was victimizing her by pilfering her trust fund. "So you willingly took in a child despite her having mental problems?"

"I am used to working with children. I was told physically she was a healthy young thing but that she witnessed a terrible three car auto accident which caused her total loss of memory. Passing Bette off as my niece was easy, telling the child she was my niece was unquestioned as she had total loss of memory and believed anything I told her."

"Well," Mr. Dodds said, "Ms. Kinkaid, seeing your mythical brother was not the father, and Bette Wellington was not your niece, who was she?"

"I was never told. The bank never said and I never cared. The money in a guaranteed trust provided an opportunity for me to live a life I never could have afforded without it so I took the position. Without it I don't know what I would have done."

Auntie Kinkaid was a verisimilitude of a saint while a confirmed sinner. Using perfunctory professional courtesy with effort, Mr. Dodds said, "I thank you for your help Ms. Kinkaid. I doubt Mr. Wellington will make an issue of the money, for now anyway, but what I must do now is find out where Bette Wellington was for the first years of her young life and what that life consisted of, it may have a bearing on her suicide."

Auntie Kinkaid supplied Mr. Dodds with the name of the bank in London and the name of Frank Evans the vice president of the trustee division who administered trust payments to Auntie Kinkaid until five years ago. Mr. Dodds was told at the London bank, Mr. Evans had retired five years ago. He was now living a pastoral life in a small hamlet near Bedford, England about two hundred miles from London. Mr. Dodds made the short flight over the Channel to Heathrow airport, the roads were paved all the way to Bedford and the traffic moved well. Arriving at four thirty in the afternoon he followed instructions obtained at the "Ole Style Pub." At the intersection of Route Seven and Bainbridge Road he found the five acre trim country residence of Frank Evans who had not aged well. He was confined to a wheelchair, had difficulty speaking clearly, only with patience and difficulty was Mr. Dodds able to learn that when Mr. Evans had his one and only meeting with the father of Bette, Mr. Evans learned he was Bishop Dexter Burling of the Anglican Diocese of St. Thomas Cathedral. When Mr. Dodds learned who the father of Bette Wellington was he said to Frank Evans, "This charlatan had a fleeting inspiration of piety that never matured, why animals exhibit greater feeling for their young than he did. What was your impression of him Mr. Evans?"

Mr. Evans wrinkled his nose. "He was imperious, cold, without any warmth or conviviality, hardly exuded any radiance you would associate with a Bishop. I was relieved when he left my office. The arrangement for the payments for his little girl were directed to me in the manner he was kenneling a dog, a most unfeeling man for a man of the clergy. My heart grieved for the little tot he was abandoning."

Dodds was a man that exhausted every possible wisp of a lead. He found the conduct of the Bishop Dexter Burling of St. Thomas Cathedral, father of Bette Wellington who deserted his child, basically abandoned her to a relative, fleeing the embarrassment attached to such a scandal the child's mysterious predicament generated was reason enough to dig further into Dexter Burling's past. Posing as a missionary who was a long time associate of Prelate Dexter Burling he discovered by piecing together bits of statements from several church members at St. Thomas Cathedral who had known Prelate Burling Dexter many years ago that he was an independently wealthy man, a scion of a wealthy family who amassed a fortune in the tea trade to India. The family lived in an opulent compound of mini estates near Briar Cliff in County Clare. Mr. Dodds was surprised not one of the parishioners spoke warmly of Prelate Burling Dexter but did speak of the good work he accomplished with their building program. Mr. Dodds thought he could find out more if he interviewed some of the Church employees who were employed when Bishop Dexter Burling administered the district and shepherded St. Thomas Cathedral. Mr. Dodds spoke with the ten current staff members, among them the cook, a maid, the maintenance man Pete Blanel, and discovered not one of them were employed here when Bishop Dexter Burling officiated at St. Thomas.

    The only person with knowledge of Bishop Dexter Burling was the former gardener, now retired, who lived in a cottage on the periphery of the cathedral's spacious grounds. Dodds spoke again with the cook at the back door obtaining instructions to the gardener's cottage. Leonard Wilkens was the only employee still on staff since Prelate Dexter Burling left abruptly thirty years ago. Mr. Dodds was given directions where the Leonard Wilkens cottage was found. It was a neat cottage on the edge of the estate in a small copse of oak trees. His grounds were as well tended as the St. Thomas grounds. Mr. Dodds with his left hand on the neat white gate, "hallowed," and waved his right hand at a man sitting in the shade on the porch of the neat appearing dwelling. Leonard Wilkens was a seventy year old man deeply sun tanned from constant outdoor work, with a wrinkled leathery weather beaten face, who still worked every day and was prideful of it. He was stooped, quite thin, wore thick glasses, had the habit of blinking frequently. He was known as a congenial, friendly man who always had time to talk.

In his friendly folksy style, Mr. Dodds inquired, "Mr. Wilkens, I was told you have the distinction of being the longest tenured worker here at St. Thomas."

Mr. Wilkens drew on his pipe, blew a stream of smoke out. "Yep, that's a true fact sir well into thirty year it be," he said with pride.

"Did you deal much directly with Prelate Burling Dexter when he was active here?"

"Heh, only sort of sir. Bishop Dexter Burling didn't deal much with any of the staff, he was too busy for us I guess. Never showed much concern for any of us really. Now our next Bishop Bannockburn always had time to pass a word with us, showed some concern for us personally, made us feel good. Bishop Dexter Burling didn't mix with us much at all. Bishop Dexter Burling liked to be invited to the big houses for hospitality, entertainment, fine dinners, important, companionship but through the domestic grapevine the word from the domestic help in the other big houses he wasn't too popular there either. But his little girl Bette was the sweetest little thing. She was kindly, courteous, and generous with everyone. You know she and my daughter Rhoda were close friends, maybe even best friends for a spell, then she went away to Marbary Academy. I couldn't afford to send my girl Rhoda there, that was the last we saw of Bette."

"My, it's peaceful around here. Has it always been this quiet? Was it always like this?"

"We have a moment or two once in a while. Well, as I was saying, Bishop Dexter

Burling wanted his daughter to attend a more prestigious exclusive school than our local prep school. Rhoda wanted to go there too, I couldn't handle the cost so after that last summer when Bette left for Marbary Academy in Devonshire they never really saw each other again and five months after Bette left she never answered another letter from my daughter, it was like the girl passed away the break was so complete. Inquiries were made to the Bishop Burling but he never answered so we never really could find out anything about what was going on with her but we heard Bette contracted a lung condition from the ventilation system in the dormitory at Marbary Academy and was taken somewhere where the climate would favor her recovery."

"Oh, where did they take her to recuperate?"

"Nobody around here ever found out. Several of us asked the Bishop about Bette and all he would say was, "She's getting along well." It was about that time the Bishop Burling up and resigned. Some said he emigrated to Australia, some said Norway, we never did find out where. We never saw or heard about Bishop Burling or Bette again. After seventy-two summers I get tired you know, then I get questionable. Some days I remember everything, today I'm wandering."

Mr. Dodds didn't want to exhaust the old man. He thanked the old man, shook hands with him and drove away. Dodds felt like the Marbary Academy through the instructors, their records, might contribute to his search for answers. He left late in the evening hoping to avoid heavy traffic. Mr. Dodds in his experience knew that when portraying a potential customer he seemed to experience much greater success in obtaining information. So now he decided to assume the role of an anxious parent seeking to place his daughter in Marbary Academy. On the way he telephoned Devonshire, made an appointment for three the next afternoon. He was surprised at the stunning Marbary campus setting back from the high cliff surrounded by manicured hedges, flower beds with a panoramic view of the ocean, a fringed backdrop of magnificent oak trees towering into the sky. It exceeded in splendor many a college campus.

Mr. Dodds entered the marble hall smelling of fresh varnish from recently redone woodwork, entered the office labeled, "REGISTRATIONS." A scholarly looking man wearing thinly wired spectacles rose to meet him, bared a broad smile of greeting, his suit was baggy, wool, well worn, but qualitative, he definitely looked pedagogical. "I understood you to say you were looking to enroll your daughter into Marbary academy? Mr. Springly I believe you said the name was."

"Yes, I see from the number of boys around this is a coed institution. Has it always been so?"

"No, the first ten years it was an all girls school. Our enrollment suffered, so to enhance the continuance of our existence we transitioned to a coed institution which proved a prudent move. We have flourished since then without endowment funds, assembled some affluent alumni who are now ardent supporters."

"Well Dr. Simpkins, I am confident of the veracity and merit of the fine academic reputation you're noted for here, from a number of people with knowledge of Marbary, but what I am concerned about is my daughter's health. You see, she has a delicate situation with her respiratory system and I must be sure your dormitory facilities are no threat to her well being."

Dr. Simpkins lowered his eyebrows, pinched his nostrils together tightened his lips, reacting like he couldn't believe what he just heard.

Mr. Dodds continued, "Have you had any cases where a student had to withdraw from Marbary for health reasons?"

Dr. Simpkins leaned back in his high backed leather chair, steepled his hands, with an attitude talking down to an absurd comment he said, "I don't know what you heard that would prompt you to ask questions of that nature, but I can assure you the dormitories are only twelve years old in perfect condition, our duct system and furnaces are all maintained by professionals. Now unless you regard a tonsillectomy, or an emergency appendectomy as withdrawals for health reasons, why then we haven't had any."

"Please forgive me for persisting doctor but the reason I brought it up was last summer at a fund raising luncheon for the Saint Thomas Cathedral two thousand people attended and it was there glowing comments of Marbary were made by several people who either had family or friends or knew of someone who attended this fine institution which is why I am interested to explore the feasibility of my daughter attending here. While a number of us were discussing Marbary a gentleman from Nottingham who had a distant cousin and an uncle who attended Marbary the entire grades from six through twelve recounted how there was some incident involving a young female student while he was in attendance. The incident was described rather ambiguously, but it was said it concluded with the girl withdrawing because of health reasons."

"What is the name of the person who told you this?"

"Well he didn't identify himself."

Dr. Simpkins exhaled a, "Humph" as if to belittle the tale and discount its credibility.

Mr. Dodds, said, "I didn't get his name but I got the name of the girl who withdrew, it was Bette Dexter. Dr. Simpkins, to reassure me would it be possible to see if there is a health connection here? It would relive me so much if I could know that."

With no apparent eagerness and a definite reluctance inherent in the slow rise from his black leather chair Dr Simpkins went to one of five credenzas butted up next to each other, addressed the one that included the letter D, opened the large front double door, checked three large volumes, then found the one he wanted. He put it on the desk between Mr. Dodds and himself, flipped over several pages, "Ah, here it is." As he read his eyes widened a bit. He completed reading the two long paragraphs, then sat back. "I recall the circumstances now, Mr. Dodds, mainly because it was only my second year here as superintendent and this did cause me to defend myself at a school board hearing. This young girl of thirteen and a half years old was not taken out of Marbary sir for health reasons, she was pregnant and I ordered her to leave. Her prompt exodus was an urgent necessity as our parents would have reacted cholericly I'm sure. Marbary brought in the local law, interrogated each boy, some twice, and not a lad was ever under any suspicion. We invited the provincial accreditation board to send an evaluation team to examine our procedures and practices to insure the well being of our boys and girls were protected which resulted in a highly favorable rating.

So you see sir this unfortunate incident was an isolated occurrence."

"By the way, where did the little girl go when you expelled her?"

Dr. Simpkins scratched his chin while he searched his recollections, "Ah yes, I believe a Dr. Pekinworth, head of our Science Department at that time, had a sister who was a medical practitioner at an institution called Heathcliff Sanatorium in Dover on the English Channel and accommodatingly accepted the child."

Mr. Dodds had what he needed. He profusely shook Dr. Simpkin's hand. "Dr. Simpkins, my trust and confidence is at a high level thanks to your kind forbearance and patience. Now I will not take up any more of your time today. Another day we can continue sir."

"That will be fine Mr. Dodds. We will be glad to accommodate your daughter, please bring her in when you feel inclined to enroll her."

They shook hands, again. Mr. Dodds found himself stunned with what he learned at Marbary. Bette Dexter was expelled from school, told to leave school, it just didn't fit the personage and character of the generous, kind, devoted niece and sweet lovable child everyone revered and adored. Dodds knew there must be more to this. He raced over a few things that bothered him, like did she have an abortion, did she have the child and if so what happened to it? Picking up his bags from his hotel room he found himself driving a brisk pace along the channel road toward Heathcliff Sanitarium in Dover. He felt there must be some personnel around that could remember something about Bette Dexter Wellington. Dodds enjoyed the two lane highway looking down on the sandy banks of the shores of the English Channel with several small sailing vessels plying near shore. Out a much greater distance were huge cargo vessels so far out that they looked just as small because of the distance.

    Descending into Dover was a pretty sight. The town was originally dependent on fishing for a livelihood, but now the evidence of the twenty-five hotels identified Dover as a tourist center. Mr. Dodds filled the tank of his car and visited a water front restaurant, "The Captains Table," for fish and chips with a tankard of ale. He'd never visited England before so when he finished his lunch he indulged in a game of darts. He did so poorly his opponent, a Cockney sailor lad, looked at Dodds with good natured humor. "Matey my lad, this isn't your game." He tossed a dart almost dead center making his point, then smiled, tipped his stein all the way up, downed the last inch of his ale, and gave a careless wave over his shoulder as he was leaving.

Detective Dodds went over his notes in his car. He remembered Dr. Simpkins at Marbary saying he was convinced Bette Burling Dexter was totally unaware of her condition. Mr. Dodds theorized that possibly that was when she lost her memory. His Eminence, unyielding unsympathetic Prelate Burling Dexter, probably grilled, badgered, unhinged the poor girl jumbling her sanity and causing loss of memory.

He pulled into the Heathcliff parking lot, into a parking space lettered, VISITORS, announced to the receptionist he would like to arrange for accommodations for his seventh month pregnant wife and was shown into the office of Dr. David Cornwallis, a dignified looking man of fifty plus. In a few minutes he informed Dodds that of the hundreds of convalescent sanitariums in southeastern England Heathcliff Sanitarium enjoyed one of the best reputations of all. "We pride ourselves on the highest standard of medical care for our patients, a staff with one of the highest ratios of registered nurses to staff, total confidentiality as many of our clients would not care for publicity." When he said that, he shot a quick look at Dodds, who gave him a mournful look.

Dodds dropped his false deception. "Dr. Cornwallis, my girlfriend is half my age. We probably will not persist in our relationship after this stay here but I do want the best for her." Dodds was playing the role of a guilty errant husband.

Dr. Cornwallis tried not to reveal a look of disdain at Dodds. Dr. Cornwallis had seen so many young girls, fine young girls corrupted by older men then thrown unceremoniously aside in brutal fashion. Dr. Cornwallis with courteous professionalism said, "Let me provide you a matron to show you our fine facilities and answer any questions you may have sir." He walked to the door, pointed to a small office across the hall. "Matron Evaline handles all our tours. Give this to Evaline Bates, she will take good care of you." Dr. Cornwallis wheeled quickly and retreated into his office lending the impression he wished to withdraw from Dodds's presence as quickly as possible.

After a quick scan of his application, Evaline Bates said, "When's the blessed event due Mr. Cringly?"

"November."

"Then I guess you'll be needing me to reserve a room for you."

Mr. Cringly toured the facility, the delivery rooms, the convalescent rooms, expressing approval of what he was seeing. Evaline was jovial, given to obesity with a pleasant demeanor equipping her for the job to put people at ease. Mr. Cringly was comfortable with her at once, he was sure part of the reason was her many years of experience in dealing with questionable pregnancies.

"The young girl I wronged is with her parents now, I mean to see her though this though."

"Well that's something anyway," attendant Evaline Bates said. "We see them come in here alone, destitute, emotionally destroyed, it's pitiful." Cringly extended a pack of cigarettes toward her, attendant Evaline Bates grabbed one, lit up, sat back puffing contently then said, "Our patrons come in nervous goose and ganders alike and feel compelled to talk to dismiss their nervousness, so let's talk Cringly." Evaline Bates listened with patience to Cringly's mythical young girlfriend in trouble, she felt it part of her job.

"What I worry about the most," Mr. Cringly said, "is the girl is barely seventeen. Although she is a plucky young one, I reassured her I will take care of all expenses, be generous without threats or legalities to do so until the child is of age."

"Well that sounds a little better than some cases we get in here. Why we have cases where not only is there no offer of financial aid but total denial of being the father. You can't imagine the devastating effect on a poor young girl then. That is tragic."

"Miss Bates is seventeen, too young for a young girl to experience mother hood?"

"Oh my no, we've had 'em a lot younger than that. In fact, doctors claim the younger they are the easier time they have of it because their bones aren't too set yet. The ones that give me the headaches are the older ones who finally conceived after trying for years then come in here happy and gleeful thinking they're in for a cake walk. We show 'em different. Your young girl into athletics?"

"Not really, she just takes a swim occasionally."

"Good, muscle bound athletes are on the average in labor much, much longer as a rule they require caesarians more often too." Evaline Bates blew three long puffs of smoke. "Yes, I can tell you all about this business. Why we have had 'em from fourteen to fifty. Mr. Cringly, would you like to see some of our babies and how carefully we tend them?"

"Yes, I surely would," Mr. Cringly said, feigning interest he didn't have. He didn't even want the tour of the facility but he felt showing interest was necessary for appearances, was prepared for what Evaline Bates was going to throw at him, he thought she liked using a little shock treatment with her tales. When he observed the mothers and babies in the wards, the commotion, the clamor, the wailing, he vowed to remain a bachelor. He thought, if Evaline Bates would be so talkative on one cigarette what could he get from her with dinner and a few

Ten Stories of Mystery – Suspense – Adventure – Intrigue

martinis? He feigned looking for a room for the fictitious Cassandra Warring, selecting a room with a direct view of the English Channel with Calais, France across the mist. Cringly even put a deposit down. Then he wondered if it were permissible to have her join him for dinner to show his appreciation for all her kind assistance with his problem. "Great, it's kind of you and I'm gratified you asked," she said.

Dodds said, "I saw near the coast the See Garden Restaurant, the Marine Port Brewery, the Port O'Plenty, the Cricketreer's Crab House, and the Sea Garden Buffet. Which sounds good to you Ms. Bates?"

"The one with the best daiquiris in town, what else? The Port O'Plenty. And please call me Evaline."

"Ok Evaline, the Port O'Plenty, it will be." They agreed to rendezvous at six forty five.

By ten fifteen, after a sumptuous lobster dinner and four daiquiris, Mr. Cringly heard hair raising tales of births, complications, emergency measures that left him agog with amazement at what went on in a convalescent sanatorium. "Evaline, you're a literary treasure of exciting tales. You should compile them and have them published. They're too good not to share them."

"I intend to do that, but only with fictitious names, you understand we're discreet here you know."

"Yes I gathered that. What was your most unique, bizarre case that would be your biggest seller?"

"Oh that's easy. We had a girl barely fourteen from apparently an affluent well to do family. The father brought her in, I believe he said the mother was deceased. He offered to pay a huge sum for us to take her but we're not ghouls here preying on people, when I told him our fees he eagerly engaged us. He was so glad to be rid of his daughter, he made it clear he was never to be contacted directly, for any reason, as he was leaving the country permanently. I wouldn't have believed he said that but I happened to be there that morning, he even gave me a generous tip. I was paid to keep her for an extra two months until he could make permanent arrangements for her as he was leaving the country permanently. Can you imagine a father leaving his young daughter intending to leave the country permanently and the child not too sound mentally in some ways?"

The bar girl came over carrying her tray, picked up two empty daiquiri glasses. Mr. Cringly held up one finger, the bar girl nodded. "Oh, and coffee for me." Evaline was off and running, couldn't stop talking now with satiation of her favorite liquor savoring in her. "Oh, how did the child get into this predicament? The father claimed it happened at a coed school. I never accepted that story, the fact was the poor little darling couldn't tell us anything about what happened. Usually after several months I get everything out of 'em, all the little details good and bad, in fact I can tell you they're glad to tell someone after a while but I never got a word from her as long as she was here. I heard her father who was some kind of clergyman who give sermons many times about how blessed and wonderful the story of the Virgin Mary was. She said this is what happened to her too."

The bar girl came over with the bill but Mr. Cringly waved her off. "You mean the girl thought this was a preternatural happening?"

"Yes, that was what she thought. Several of us patiently told her the details of the facts of life, but she couldn't be swayed. She told attendant Mimi Dirkin that these things did happen, but only to other girls it definitely couldn't happen to her. She said she had often dreamed of angels so probably one came to visit her on this glorious mission. She said her father would be sorry, disapproving, not realizing this was to be the new savior. You know it was heartbreaking to hear this sweet child talk with such confidence and faith that this will happen. She told us all more than once how she loved children but expressed great anxiety whether or not she was good enough to be the mother of the new savior. Mimi Dirkin, myself, and most of the other staff became so fond of the baby. It was so beautiful, a perfectly featured little doll that I must confess actually looked sanctified but I of course didn't believe it. When she held it, it looked like an animated little doll in her arms. The next day several of us were standing by her bed visiting her. We loved the darling sweet innocent girl even though we knew she was astray mentally. Mimi Dirkin said, "Look at that sweet baby, he's a black Norman Curlycue isn't he?" That's for sure, a reference to the influx of black Normans from France after William the Conqueror vanquished King Harold at the battle of Hastings in 1066 and do you know that's what he became, our little black Norman Curlycue from then on. The girls at work and I never saw a more devoted doting mother. Some of the girls who gave birth were bitter, some didn't want the child, some were regretful, but not this sweet child. She thought she was the luckiest girl in the world. Mimi Dirkin asked me to switch days with her so I was working on a Monday. I said, "Good morning princess, how's the black Norman Curlycue?" "Oh Evaline," she said, looking down at her beautiful baby, "why was I blessed to do this, why was I sanctified so," then she wept with happiness. I've seen everything in all the years I have been at Heathcliff and I'm not vulnerable to emotions but I almost sobbed and so did Julie Evers, the other counselor on duty. I don't ever want to see the suffering that child went through then."

"What do you mean?"

"Well, two weeks later the Bishop Dexter Burling called and announced he was leaving the country and he had made provisions for Bette and of course she couldn't carry on with her life with a baby not much younger than herself so they had to be separated. They were already together over three weeks which is much too long. The girls and I decided there was only one thing we could do, so the following morning we told Bette the child died of complications during the night. When she heard he died she gave a long shrieking scream that to my dying day I will forever be haunted by it. Then she lapsed into unconsciousness for so long it was more like a coma. We were so worried we called a doctor from the local hospital. He said the shock of losing her baby caused the coma and it was possible might have some after effects from losing it. And do you know what? When she came to that afternoon she didn't know me, or Mimi, or Julie Evers. When her father came to pick her up she didn't know him either, she had completely lost her memory. The doctor from the hospital said she was healthy and sound in every way, but was suffering apparently from total amnesia, shock or comatose, and only time and analysis would reveal which. The girls and I felt it was merciful it happened, we didn't think she could have handled losing her baby. We thought waking up to that fact would have driven her insane."

Dodds felt he heard all he needed to, waved to the bar girl for the bill, paid it, tipped the girl generously for her attentive service. Dodds could see Evaline was emotionally affected just from relating the tragic story, "Thank you for the details Evaline. I think if you write your memoirs this story should be your center piece. By the way, what happened to her baby?"

Evaline said, "I have a cousin who is a gym teacher at St Albert's orphanage near Croydon, whom we cooperate with quite closely so we sent him there. We called him Robert Folsom, but to us girls at Heathcliff he will always be the black Norman Curly-cue."

Dodds kept up his false identity as Mr. Cringly saying, "As soon as I return I will tell you what date I will bring the young woman in so you can reserve her room." Telling sincere sounding falsehoods was part of the detective persona that Dodds had accepted long ago.

He felt another session with Leonard Wilkens might yield more information as he was a contemporary of Bishop Burling for years. Perhaps there was something he forgot to tell him last time or there was something he remembered since their last visit. When he pulled up to the gardener's cottage a woman was just coming out with an eleven year old girl behind her and a little baby in her arms. "Good morning miss. I'm here to see Mr. Leonard Wilkens, is he around?"

The woman smiled, "My dad's not here. I'm his daughter Mrs. Rhoda Faraday. This is my daughter Rosalinda."

"Pleasure miss."

"You just missed him. He's off to pick up some new hedges at Sussex."

"What time will he be back?"

She laughed, "Who knows? If he runs into his cronies he may be gone for the day, even two, they do like their cups you know."

Mr. Dodds looked around, just like last time he visited Leonard Wilkens he was impressed with the stillness. "It seems so serene and peaceful around here."

"Yes, this is a quiet orderly community except when the shearers come down to help with the shearing it sometimes gets a bit rowdy."

"Interesting, I didn't know they brought in temporary help for that."

"Oh yes, there isn't enough local labor available around here you know. There's mostly gentry in the area, they are not in need of the employment. The transients are quite a rambunctious lot, quite lively at times. They're from the poorest sections of the towns you know."

"Then I guess you local folks wouldn't have much to do with them particularly the young girls around here like your daughter here."

She looked sternly at her daughter. "She knows what would happen to her back side if she's even seen talking to one of the shearers."

"Why Ma, just because you were silly one time?"

Rhoda Faraday shifted her child to her other arm, laughed, "Yes, you're right honey. I was foolish one time when I was your age. I never told you the story, you're old enough now so you'll understand why I forbid you any contact with them. When I was twelve my childhood girlfriend and I were told not to have anything to do with the shearers too but Bette and I..."

"Oh," said Mr. Dodds, "Bette who?"

"Why Bette Dexter Burling, my best childhood friend."

"Oh, you mean they caused you a problem?"

"Almost. We were ordered to stay away from them," Rhoda Byron snickered. "We were told more than once not to go near them but we did sneak out once in a while to see them. I guess because they were different. Bette and I even got to know one of the families who seemed nicer than the others. Once they were having a party, I don't remember exactly but I think it was an anniversary celebration. Several of the boys took us off to the woods and gave us lager to drink. It was good. Towards the last they gave us something stronger and we both got groggy, silly, quite dizzy, neither of us remembered that night nor much of the next day either. If my dad would have found out he would have thrashed me good, and Bette's father the Bishop Burling would have excommunicated her," she said with sardonic humor.

She shifted her baby from one arm to the other again. Mr. Dodds sensed her struggle juggling her baby. Her daughter Rosalinda saying again, "Ma, can we go home now? I got to go to work at the dairy."

Mr. Dodds considerately thanked Mrs. Byron, tickled the baby under the chin with a smile, leaned over, patted the young slender Rosalinda on the head. "Sorry for delaying you for work young lady. Thank you Mrs. Faraday, here's my card with cell phone if you think of anything at all please call me." Then he tickled the baby under the chin, gave a valedictory wave to the mother and daughters, got in his car and headed back to his hotel. After he arrived at his hotel Mr. Dodds reviewed his notes and determined he had followed all possible leads in England so he booked a flight back to Effingham, Illinois.

On arrival in Effingham he immediately visited Detective Marino at the Effingham Police Department to find out if any new information had been discovered about Mrs. Wellington's suicide. The detective informed him a salesman had recently been to the residence and was in conference in the study with Bette Wellington when the maid brought in coffee. She mentioned Bette Wellington handing over cash to the salesman. The salesman had left a catalogue with Bette Wellington when he left, there was no order slip or receipt left behind indicating Mrs. Wellington had purchased anything, yet Dodds noted the maid had said she saw while pouring coffee that Mrs. Wellington had passed money to the salesman. Dodds called the phone number on the catalogue of the Rembrandt Lawn and Garden Company in Boca Raton, Florida who informed Mr. Dodds they had a regional office in Chicago, Illinois who might have the identity of the salesman he sought. Driving north from Effingham, Mr. Dodds was starting to feel the cause of this tragic suicide may never be discovered and commiserated with the suffering Mr. Wellington, but he was determined to file a complete report and this seemed to be the last avenue to find an answer that he had left.

    Mr. Dodds called at the regional office of the Rembrandt Lawn and Garden Company. He spoke to the manager, Ben Welkowski, explained his identify and mission, and that his salesman had been the last person besides the butler to see the woman in the news that was a suicide. "Wow," said the manager. "Well, he doesn't come into the office too often, he is on the road a lot, but he's in town now. You can try him at home, here's his name and address. Hope he's not in trouble, seems like he's ok."

Dodds, with his customary thoroughness asked, "Did Sheldon Dark sell anything to Mrs. Wellington?"

"Well, let me check his recorded orders." He sat down at his computer. "No, apparently not."

Dodds didn't comment, except a "Thank you."

He rang the doorbell at 4854 West Belden in a twelve flat building in a middle class neighborhood in Chicago. When Sheldon Dark opened the door Dodds was startled with Sheldon Dark's anomalous combination of lustrous, black, shiny dark hair with masses of ringlets of hair, all over his head, on the sides, on the nape of his neck, all uniform making a pleasing symmetrical picture, a combination Dodds never saw before. The young man was taller than Dodds, had a thin nose, medium build, a cherubic guileless looking face incompatible with his felonious character, but a pleasing face compatible with the sales craft profession and a perfunctory amiable attitude he employed when utilizing salesmanship. He had a narrow pinched face. Dodds raised a card to present him with, "This is my card sir. As you can see, I'm with the detective agency hired by the husband of the woman in the news who committed suicide recently."

"Oh, I see, yes I called there. I remember her, left some literature, then left. That was it."

"Anything unusual happen that you can think of?"

"No that's it. Nothing else happened that I can think of."

Dodds enjoyed toying with someone he knew he had cornered as a liar and a thief. "It seems there's a witness who says otherwise."

Sheldon Dark began looking at Dodds suspiciously and with wariness. "Why, are you accusing me of something?"

"Your name is not Sheldon Dark is it?"

Then Sheldon Dark collapsed, shedding his cover. "Alright, I took an order, asked her to make out a check to me personally, strictly for convenience you understand, I didn't mean to keep the money."

Dodds thought of how Auntie Kinkaid lied to cover up her embezzlement, thought of how Burling Dexter lied about why he resigned, why he abandoned a young daughter whose mind he disoriented with intensive questioning for which she had no mortal answers. "Why are you not using your correct name?"

Mr. Dodds expected a familiar name, Ronald Folsom, to be mentioned but instead Sheldon Dark with downcast eyes said, "My name is Terrence Belemy."

Mr. Dodds was confused, he wasn't sure if he was hearing the truth, or a denial, so he pressed on. Terrence Belemy had no trace of an English accent whatsoever. "Where are you from Terrence?"

"I transferred to Chicago from Boca Raton, Florida a year ago."

"Now Terrence, you know whatever you say to me will be confirmed at the Rembrandt Lawn and Garden Company. I am investigating a murder, so the police will run a complete investigation on you. It would look better for you if you told the truth now so be cautious with your answers."

"I suggest to you Mr. Dark or Belemy you tell your firm up front what you did, it might look better for you. If you do I will not report this irregularity to your company."

The young man looked distressed, but relieved. His brow was wrinkled with worry. "Ha," he said, "I knew you came from the firm. I might have known it, everyone's been against me it seems. Why I just saw an opportunity to pick up some extra money for myself, that's all, I meant no bad intentions, I swear. But when I saw on the news the woman killed herself I thought I could pull it off."

"Pull off what?"

"You know, cash her check and spend the money, doctor my order book, say nothing about anything. I try one darn thing to help myself and I get nailed, nothing works for me." He launched into a self pitying soliloquy of how this is how it's always been, he's never had a chance.

Mr. Dodds smiled to himself. He thought Sheldon Dark was kind to himself to use the euphemism, "no bad intentions" instead of the correct word "theft." When his laments turned into whining Dodds thought disdainfully if this was the destined savior of the world, then his thoughts turned to itinerant shearers, anniversaries, temporary shanties, sheep shearing sheds, beer, ales, strong lager, adventuress girls, and a sneaky, lustful black haired boy like this one skulking around.

"You're sure you won't tell my company on me if I answer what you want to know?"

"That's what I said."

"Well what are your questions then?"

"What is your legal name?"

The troubled young man took a deep breath, "Terrence Belemy."

"Where were you born?"

"Weymouth, England."

"Oh, isn't that across from Le Havre, France?"

"No sir, it's across from Cherbourg."

"I see. Were you ever in Dover?"

"No sir, never went that far west."

"How long have been in this country?"

"Four years."

"You have no trace of an English accent, why is that?"

"The district manager of my company suggested sales would be easier if I could speak proper English without a foreign accent, and you know he was right."

"Ever heard of Heathcliff Sanatorium?"

"No sir."

"Ever heard of St. Alberts Orphanage?"

"No."

Mr. Dodds was thoroughly convinced that Terrence Belemy was a happenstance that just came along. "Now I have to ask you this and I advise you to answer with the utmost thought as to the consequences not to. Why are using the name Sheldon Dark instead of your real name Terrence Belemy?"

Terrence Belemy adopted a sheepish look of reluctance in his face pursing his lips in brief speculation, then remembered Mr. Dodds promised not to inform his company of his impropriety with Bette Wellington's order if he told the complete truth. He sighed deeply, "Well, back in my hometown of Weymouth, England there is a court summons for me to appear to answer for a battery charge brought against me, and knowledge of that by my company would have finished me with them so I changed names to prevent being found, fired, served and extradited."

Mr. Dodds smiled, "Probably a good idea, but it's unlikely for a relative misdemeanor like that for an extradition proceeding to be put into play."

Terrence Belemy looked surprised, with a pleased expression.

"Terrence, would you go over in detail one more time exactly everything that occurred when you spoke with Bette Wellington?"

"Well," he resumed, "I always called at the fancy houses. Most I couldn't get into but I knew when I did the orders were big. When I called at that lady's house an English maid answered and because she sensed I was English from a word here and there she asked if her mistress would see me and it so happened she had interest in my line and I got an audience with her. I showed the lady several brochures. She picked eight items, a pretty good sized order I may add and that's all there was to it, I swear."

"Hold on a moment," said Dodds. "Was Mrs. Wellington courteous to you, did she make a fuss over you in any way?"

"What? No, why should she? I'm nobody."

Dodds pursued the questioning, "Did she say anything in particular to you?"

"Not really, just looked at my brochures, said she thought they were beautiful and ordered. Then I asked her to make out the check to me personally, that's it. One thousand and eighty dollars it was. I felt I was finally doing something for myself."

Mr. Dodds lit a cigarette. "The first opportunity you got, you used it to steal. Don't you feel terrible about that?"

"No, only about getting caught at it," then he laughed. "I'll to be smarter next time I guess."

So much for young people saving the world thought Dodds. Dodds took a close look at Terrence Belemy, a young man with tainted morals and ethics then thought about the pious, sweet Bette Wellington and her saintly past and wondered about the unreliability of genetics. Dodds thanked the young man, walked to his car, left to report to Mr. Wellington.

Dodds had some strong ideas of what had occurred but nothing really concrete to satisfy a grieving husband. The butler opened the door, Dodds entered, as a last inspiration Dodds again went over each detail with what he saw, heard and knew of the young salesman that was the last to see Mrs. Wellington alive other than the maid. He learned nothing in addition to what he learned from him before. While reviewing his notes a long distance call from the Chicago Police Department homicide division came in. They wanted to know where to mail or fax the report on Terrence Belemy, A.K.A. Sheldon Dark. Mr. Dodds didn't believe in miracles and he didn't get one, the name he expected didn't materialize, it was too much to expect. When Mr. Dodds left Terrence he had increased sympathy for Bette and Jon Wellington, he knew he must reveal a conclusion to Jon Wellington soon. He went home, called his old friend Dr. Blemquist to make an appointment. Thinking over a few points he wanted to pursue with his friend Dr. Blemquist, Mr. Dodds, seeing the Cockney maid was the last person to see Mrs. Wellington alive, decided on one more review of her comments. "Brenda, when you came in with the coffee for your mistress, after you showed the young salesman out, Mrs. Wellington rang again and asked you for more cream, is that right?"

"Yes sir, then the butler came in again while I was there. I heard him ask her if she wanted the chauffer available and she declined saying her husband was taking her to the movies in the afternoon."

"Made no reference or comment about the salesman that just left at all?"

"No sir, she didn't say a thing, but I did say as I was leaving the room, I don't think Mrs. Wellington heard me, but I said to the butler, "If that young salesman ever showed up again I would know him because of his black Norman curlyque ringlets. "Then I resumed my dusting duties in the library."

"I see, thank you Brenda."

Dodds checked his notes from beginning to end again. He saw the statements of medical counselors at Heathcliff Sanatorium who repeatedly referred to Bette's baby as, "the black curlycue Norman," then matched it up with Brenda's comment of the, "black curlycue Norman," and dwelled on the psychiatric possibilities then read on.

Dodds thought he had an idea of what the mystery of Bette Wellington's apocalyptic suicide was motivated by, but without additional medical confirmation he dared not make a conclusion he had no well defined acts or motives to deal with and felt must be analyzed by a qualified authority in the field so he contacted an old professional colleague.

Dodds thought with Bette Wellington's loss of memory, her emotional galvanic response to being told her baby was dead might have the secret of her suicide concealed in the recesses of her mind with that thought he went to his appointment with his old colleague Dr. Blemquist hoping some light would be shed on the conundrum of Bette Wellington's suicide.

He joined Dr. Blemquist in his office the following night. The office was in bright colors, comfortable furniture, but otherwise in a Spartan atmosphere. There was an elaborate electronic system to provide mood music to relax patients, and even a wet bar concealed behind the large credenza if refreshments were needed. "Please sit down Dodds."

"Thanks Hank, it's been a while."

"Yep, about a year I make it."

Dodds had sent all the particulars a week before so Dr. Blemquist could have time to analyze the facts. "Find anything enlightening Hank?"

"I can't say I found anything concrete, but I can say specifically what I didn't find may be of some help."

Dodds fastened his attention on Blemquist, watching him turn to his first page of notes.

"From the memos and statements on her childhood Dodds, there was never any evidence of compulsive personality disorders. She was kind to all, sociable, with agreeable traits. Her profile exhibits no paranoid tendencies, was trusting, mutually respectful of others despite suffering the loss of her beloved child. Nowhere could I find any schizoid indications or complications. I definitely can rule out any histrionic disorders. Also ruled out is any passive aggressive tendencies, nowhere is this even hinted at, along with the complete absence of anti social conduct. Being un-indulged in sexual activity, before and after what must have happened to her apparently unknowingly, the blocking out of the incident or the total non-recognition of the occurrence rules out any psychosexual character disorders as confirmed here by all who knew her as a child and her intimate guardian who was a close companion. Psychogenic amnesia may occur without organic cause as a response to excessive stress. It tends to appear suddenly from the subject wishing insulation against pain and suffering from a remembrance. Psychogenic amnesia screens out the pain and suffering the recollection is causing, it's a bodily defense mechanism. The significant thing to consider here Dodds is that while the painful trauma may be effectively blocked out, even for years, it is capable of re-igniting in days, months, years, or decades even, instantaneously."

"Hank is it possible to identify the things that might trigger recovery of memory?"

Dr. Blemquist rubbed the corner of his mouth with his forefinger a few times. "Well let's see, the triggering stimulus could emerge in the form of a loved one, a cliché, a long lost family member, a kiss from a former intimate, from a favorite object, a memento, a relic, a nickname, a poem, a song, musical instrument, a picture, a description of a loved one, but in addition to the answer to your question Dodds, remember along with a galvanic recovery of memory suddenly is instant accompanying of the pain, the abhorring, unwanted memory that caused the subject to flee from conscious reality in the first place. The emergence may be joyous and pleasing, however, be aware Dodds no one can predict with confidence what exactly occurs when emergence is triggered, most cases vary. The dormant memory may be eliminated or it may be not only latent but potentially worse." Dodds shook his head slightly a few times thinking he heard things that may be helpful. "Dodds, a long term case stretching decades like this one is the most unpredictable because no one knows the real facts except the subject. I hope I've been of some help Dodds."

Dodds thanked Dr. Blimquist, left deeply in thought, thinking he has some unselfish conscience to awaken in himself. He was so spent physically and mentally from this case he meant to take at least a few days to finalize his findings for Mr. Jon Wellington, the aggrieved husband.

Jon Wellington came into the study. "Oh Dodds, I just heard you arrived. I hope I haven't kept you waiting. You've been here a while."

"Yes sir I was sir, just reconfirming a few points with the domestic help that's all."

"What is your conclusion then?"

Dodds at that moment made a decision to be merciful to this fine man at the expense of his professional reputation. He pretty much thought he had a good idea of things stitched together from clues here, comments there, it seemed substantial to his experienced mind now fortified with the testimony of Dr. Blemquist. Dodds wondered whether it would be preferable not to be professionally candid and tell Jon Wellington that his wife suffered delusions and hallucinations and not inform Jon Wellington that it appears a child was impregnated without conscious knowledge while drinking with boys, then fantasizing in giving birth to the new messiah of the world, then mercifully never discovering her son was not the spiritual deliverer of her thoughts and desires a product of her own, goodness, sweetness, sanctity, then abandoned by a charlatan cleric when a defenseless, innocent tot. What good would it do but only add painful memories, wrenching compassion for the man, causing him to commiserate over her tortured childhood, tarnish the sanctified image he had of her benefiting no one, not Bette Wellington, not Jon Wellington and certainly not Dodds himself.

Swallowing his professional pride in being able to solve mysteries, Mr. Dodds magnanimously stated to Mr. Wellington, "Evidence leads to the cause of suicide being a cumulative series of psychological causes induced from suppressions in childhood of denial of accepting the reality of lack of affection and condemnation from her father resulting from his remorseless interrogation, insecurities being compelled to face a world without a parent. When a child is relentlessly mentally pressed repeatedly that can cause a series of psychotic childhood anomalies that were never allowed to be expressed and identified which created a latent threat that could be ignited without warning, without reason, without any preceding aberrant behavior or warning of its existence. This induced loss of memory as a protective device of the mind to avoid the failure of her mind to correlate realty and the unexplainable. Mr. Wellington, the cumulative series of childhood depressions were unleashed on the poor woman's mind in an avalanche that was overwhelming and in a desperate defense to avoid unbearable pain she had to find escape."

    Mr. Wellington looked at Dodds. "Oh, my God, my poor, dear wife."

Jon Wellington got the general idea of what the report said, the facts now paled into oblivion and the reality now could be faced, his wife was not a victim of foul play. So far Jon Wellington was in denial about her death, now he could face the fact that his beloved wife Bette Wellington was now only a revered memory.

Dodds gathered his papers and left the grief stricken silent man to his mourning. With a clear conscience Dodds felt that he had served his client well, of having done the right thing not only for Jon Wellington, but for himself too.

The Sabbatical

Mildred and I parted that morning following the usual routine we followed every morning for twenty-five long years. She left her second cup of coffee sitting while she accompanied me to the front door. There she asserted her dominance over me by plucking a minute invisible touch of lint from my lapel, issued her usual litany of instructions for the day... don't forget to stop at the cleaners, pay our bill at the butchers, pick up some 60 watt bulbs, a package of double AA batteries, and a new broom and dust pan. She perfunctorily pecked me on the cheek. Mildred Agnus Cunningham Higgins thus sent me, Alfred Charley Higgins, off to the public accounting firm of Higgins & Associates. There were no associates, I was sole owner and proprietor of the firm that specialized in corporate taxes. Each morning this trite ritual of separation was performed without any variety or change in the tedious ceremony we engaged in, it had long ago passed from boredom to displeasure for Charley. Oh, not the conjugal partnership with his wife Mildred, oh no they were still compatible in every way, still enjoying their same mutual pleasures, but it was the peripheral things that crept up on Al without his full consciousness and it's creeping gnawing effect on him.

When I left the house that morning I had no hint or forewarning that I would suffer the affliction I did. I had not missed a day at work in fifteen years. My doctor, a general practioner, Dr. Beldorf, had cautioned me the last three years that my chemical analysis showed warning signs and advised me many times to relax more and take it easy or I would come down with something and now though I was unaware something surely was happening.

As I was walking to the L station I was thinking of Dr. Beldorf's words, but I was feeling as well or better than I usually did for no reason I could logically explain. My first symptom of irregular condition was falling asleep on the L train. I had never in my life ever done that before. I awoke on the train about forty minutes later, stunned that I had done that, I had never done that before. I thought I would get a paper when I left the L train and I realized I had no small change. When I groped for my wallet I realized I didn't have it, I had no credit cards, no I.D., but in my upper inside suit coat pocket I found 2,500 dollars in a roll of bills. I couldn't think of why they should be there.

The L train pulled into the Wells and Washington stop and without reason or logic I walked down the L stairs to the street, saw the entrance to the Regal Hotel crowded with men talking, laughing, greeting each other, it seemed so pleasant. I penetrated the crowd intending to pass up the street when a man turned on me and pumped my hand. "Greetings brother, this is my first convention, yours too?"

It wasn't natural at all but it seemed natural to answer, "Yes, mine too."

The man was quite tall, neat, mustached, bespectacled with wire framed glasses, a Brooks Brothers natty suit. "I'm from Elmira, New York, Brock Linders." He pushed out his hand and I shook it again.

From nowhere I said, "I'm Willard Pendleton from Cayuga Falls, Montana." My mind swirled wondering if I was factual and correct, I wasn't sure, just suspicious.

"Well let's register then Willie."

At the registration desk we paid the five hundred dollar fee covering room, dinner, dues, were assigned to room fourteen fifty. When vagaries infect a person's behavior it is not always evident that there is not a wide gap from illusion to hallucination. At nine o'clock that night the dinner was excellent, filet minion with tasty blandishments and selections of drinks which I drank liberally of Brandy Alexanders. The speeches were mercifully short. There were ten occupants at our table, all apparently men of attainments. John Howard was a man from Hartford, Connecticut sitting on my left. "Did you guys read about the Harvard professor that was missing six months?"

The man across the table laughed, "Ya, I did, he turned up in Tahiti living in a bamboo hut with a beauteous native girl."

"Figures," said a balding man, "what excuse did this drop out give for what happened?"

The man next to him said, "I can tell you without you saying it, probably the usual, aphasia or amnesia."

"Bingo," said the first man.

The portly cigar puffing man next to him said, "Now isn't that an impulsive conclusion not knowing if there was any degree of brain damage or not?"

Another voice chimed in, "Most aphasia cases are extremely mild, it's only when there is some kind of physical damage is acute aphasia present where loss of speech or understanding logic is a condition."

"What are you saying then?"

"I'm saying that research shows that many of these drop out cases are questionable and auto induced by the subject to escape an orderly established rat race that represents entrapment to a subject and this dropping out is an escape, a refuge. It may be temporary relief from all the contributing things that cause it, job pressure, daily routine demands, boring little repetitious requirements that have reached a point of resistance that a subject finds it desirable to avoid for a while to be able to regroup and face things anew."

"Look guys, I didn't come to this convention to talk shop, let's go down to the hotel bar."

Several of the men went with him. Willard Pendleton left the convention room and headed to the men's wash room towards the end of the hall. As he was passing the next doorway where a wedding was in full progress with a five piece band, dancing, drinking, well wishing, a table with a huge mound of wedding gifts, a Conga line was in process. From just inside the doorway a melodious voice sang out, "Why Alfred Charles Higgins, you bad boy, you weren't going to pass me by without a word?" she admonished. In confusion Willard Pendleton shook her hand. "You didn't recognize me Al?"

"Why I ah, I ah...."

"I'm little Rosy Pritchard, remember? I know it's been years, but some things people can never forget, don't tell me you have." She fluttered her eyelashes to indicate some degree of intimacy having been shared by them in the past. "Oh by the way, is Marian here? I'd like to say hello."

Willard Pendleton didn't answer for a few moments and then he blurted out, "That's just it, I have forgotten everything. You see, I am Willard Pendleton from Cayuga Falls, Montana."

Rosy rolled skeptical eyes towards her lady friend laden with suspicion. Ignoring his claim to his alien identity she said, "Oh Al, you know I was married six months after you and Marian moved from St. Paul. I would like you to meet my husband Frank."

Anxious to escape, Willard Pendleton excused himself with the insincere promise to return, visited the wash room then went to his hotel room, checked out, went two blocks down and checked into the Embassy Hotel. He asked himself why he did that but received no answer. He then went to a Stouffer's restaurant, dined, visited their elegant bar and met a young woman, Beverly Aikens, a young attractive ambitious girl who professed a burning desire to earn tuition for the next term at Concordia College in nursing training.

Willard awoke the next morning as the ambitious girl with such a strong desire to heal that she was apparently willing to make any effort to get there. Alfred watched intently as she was slipping into her panties. Willard felt virile and bold as his visible physical reaction grew and grew, then when the future healer asked him if he would be gentleman enough to fasten her bra for her, his hands cupped her fine, firm breasts. He timidly inquired if she would accept another donation to her educational fund. She thought it would be most charitable of him to advance her educational efforts so instead of fastening her bra Willard removed it and Beverly Aikens rewarded her benefactor with an extra half an hour allowing him to donate an additional $200 toward her intended medical tuition.

Willard didn't really have anything planned for that day or night. He loved the spontaneity, doing what he felt like when he felt the whim, no schedule, no deadline, no urgent deliveries of documents. For no explicit reason and no thorough thought he purchased two tickets to the current play at the Schubert Theater, "Les Miserables," then he retired to his room, allowed room service to pamper him for several hours with snacks and drinks, relaxed, watched TV for an hour, slept two more hours, and finally felt physically restored from his charitable exertions.

He went to Anderson's Sea Food restaurant on Erie and State near Navy Pier and met a Molly Shanahan, a voluptuous, enticing deceptively modestly garbed young women who lo and behold related the tragic sudden loss of her mother three weeks ago, lost her job at the computer rental firm two weeks ago, and now was assiduously seeking employment to save for a new wheelchair for her father whom she said no longer was able to work. Willard was not normally a cynical person but neither was he credulous either. "Well Molly," Willard empathized, "I am not an employer but I would be delighted if you would join me for a lobster dinner. It may be that talking to someone will ease your pain and cheer you up."

After detailed discussions on a variety of subjects, Willard Pendleton concluded Molly Shanahan's mind had not kept pace with her curvaceous, provocative body, despite the unadorned, plain clothing she displayed she still exuded an overwhelming presence. Willard found when he suggested she might enjoy the play "Les Miserables" at the Schubert, he was amazed it was the one play she said that she always wanted to see but never had the opportunity. Willard magnanimously accepted the coincidence.

The crowd came streaming out of the first act into the lobby at the Schubert for intermission, "I say hello, Higgins, haven't seen or heard of you since you moved from Harlem and North in Forest Park to Barrington. How's Marian? Is she here?" he said, as he surveyed the desirous young girl at Willard's side.

Willard Pendleton lifted his head up, "Sir you mistake me, I am Willard Pendleton from Cayuga Falls, Montana. Now if you will pardon us," and he escorted Molly Shanahan briskly towards a settee in the corner to sip their refreshments. As the man and his astonished wife retreated Willard Pendleton heard the word, "Disgraceful."

Willard Pendleton was amazed that sweet, innocent looking young Molly Shanahan could give such sublime pleasures in assorted variety, it was paradisiasical beyond words to describe it. To soothe her sorrows at losing her mother and her job she allowed me to force $200 dollars on her to demonstrate the sincerity of my profound sympathy. The unfortunate, but talented young girl who spun dreams for the fortunate left at nine o'clock in the morning hinting lightly she was still despondent and had no plans. Willard of Cayuga Falls, Montana wanted no schedules, no appointments, ignored the feelers. I slept until eleven o'clock, tired from my body's eager responses to Molly Shanahan's tutorial enticements.

I can't give a reason why, but as soon as Molly left I headed down to the desk to check out and intended to log in at another hotel. What was the reason? I didn't know, but thought I should. As I approached the desk I saw the desk clerk huddled with a tall portly man who briefly pointed in my direction. The man was in a black suit, wearing a derby with a black string tie hanging in conformance with his huge bulging, protruding paunch. He advanced a step toward me, blocking my passage. I looked up startled. "Yes sir, what is it you want?"

At that moment a woman rushed past the tall man in black brushing in front of him shouting, "Alfred, Alfred, don't you know me? I'm your dutiful loving wife. Tell me it's alright Alfred, please."

She threw her arms up around my neck causing me to choke and gag momentarily. I firmly and deliberately removed her hands from around my neck and looked at her with detached indifference. "Madame, I apologize for my deceptive appearance but mistaken identity has been my malady these last few days."

Dr. Beldorf grasped the woman firmly by putting his arm around her and holding one arm firmly with his other hand while he led the distraught, sobbing woman out of the lobby. As they were moving slowly away I heard, "Mildred, I will talk to him. I may be able to help, after all, I've treated Al for 20 years. Insane? Absolutely not. Maybe amnesia or slight aphasia, we can determine this better when we can give him a thorough physical and mental examination."

Dr. Beldorf returned appeared before Willard Pendleton sitting on the divan in the hotel lobby monitored by Detective Hollander who was smoking another large cigar with his derby at a cockish angle. "Mr. Pendleton, may I have a word with you sir?"

"Why yes, certainly."

Dr. Beldorf said in a firm authoritative voice, "First, let's set your mind straight on something right off. Your name is definitely Albert Charles Higgins, a successful owner of a profitable C.P.A. firm specializing in corporate taxes, and your name is definitely not Willard Pendleton and you're definitely not from Cayuga Falls, Montana."

"I am well aware of that sir, but a man can't go around without giving a name when asked to, and I don't particularly have any attraction for the name Pendleton but it seemed to do."

"Yes, yes, I see your problem Al. Since I have been your physician for over twenty years, I advised you to ease up on more than one occasion, but you ignored my advice, over burdened yourself, lapsing into amnesiac aphasia hopefully mild, fleeting and temporary. That fine looking woman who was here a moment ago is your dutiful, loving wife who has been under my constant care for the past two and a half weeks, unable to sleep or eat properly and under medication. We picked up your whereabouts when we received telegrams from two people who were convinced they spoke with you. Despite your use of an alias they were convinced it was you. You know Al, we have been friends since we roomed at Penn State together, I was best man at your wedding."

I said, "I'm feeling tired, I must lie down," and I stretched out on the long divan in the hotel lobby as Doctor Beldorf leaned over, explaining he came with Mildred as soon they got a line on my location.

"Now Al, try to remember, try hard, by intense concentration memories are jogged into place, in some cases it takes a little longer."

After a few minutes of frowning and wearing an appearance of futility, I said, "It's not working. Is this amnesiac aphasia able to be treated?"

"Well, when someone lapses into this affliction the cure can be speedy or prolonged."

I got up from the divan in the lobby, looked at an attractive blond haired girl with a low cut dress, then drifted my gaze to a young woman standing by the elevator thinking how neither of them could compare to Molly Shanahan or the artistic Beverly Aikens.

Dr. Beldorf resumed, "Sometimes the recovery progresses slowly, but steadily, sometimes speedily, sometimes instantly, sometimes only gradual improvement, then relapses, each case is unique Al."

"Hmm, well then will you see me through this?"

"My good friend I will summon all my medical skills to assist your recovery."

"Oh that's a relief, I feel weary from it all." I lay down on the divan again, closed my eyes living my sixteen days all over again vicariously. Without opening my eyes I said, "It will be best Robby old friend to have an expeditious recovery without delay. You can go now and bring Mildred in, if you wish, but Robby, good old Robby, it was spectacular," and playfully punched him on his upper arm accompanied with a wink.

Perspicacity

Trixie Catrell hurried across the lawn behind the trim brick two story, five room home shaded by four huge oak trees to her visiting sister Gloria Jean with a beaming smile on her round, plump face. "Gloria Jean!" she shouted, "Myrtle Jenkins just got off the phone, and who do suppose is visiting her brother Rex for a week?"

Sitting in the shade in a wicker lawn chair Gloria Jean's left hand was holding a glass of ice tea in mid air sipping it alternately while paging an advanced algebra book in her lap with her right hand. Considering the question rhetorical Gloria Jean said, "Ok, I'll bite, who?"

"Lomax Reeding, that's who." Trixie watched for any perceptible reaction at all. This told Trixie very little as Gloria Jean was never one to display any visible emotions. "I wonder, would you mind seeing him again."

Gloria Jean flipped another page of advance algebra over, with an indifferent shrug she said, "No matter."

"You wouldn't mind then if he visited here."

"It's insignificant to me one way or another." The answer was terse, direct, an answer from a self assured woman who was accustomed to living alone for several years now.

"Oh Gloria Jean, that's wonderful, because I've invited him."

Gloria sipped her ice tea, "Does he know I'm visiting you?"

"Well I didn't talk with Lomax directly, but I made a point of mentioning to Myrtle you were here for a week so he'll know you're still single, and when he heard you were here he said he'd enjoy visiting with us. I don't mind telling you Gloria I'm anxious to see how he looks after all these years, you know he was so handsome and sought after."

"Yes I know after all we were engaged once you know, I'm a little curious too to see how he looks."

Trixie looked at her sister's classical looking face, thinking how well she carried her thirty-two years so lightly and yet never had married. Trixie looked endearingly at her sister, Gloria Jean, then put her hand over her sister's, "After all these years can you tell me what happened? You were never in love with anyone else, the rumor is Lomax never married either." Trixie thought of Gloria Jean's solitary life, then thought of how desolate her own life would be if she didn't have her two girls, Betty nine, Gloria ten, named after Auntie Gloria, and William Jr. eleven, together with her devoted husband Bill she would be miserable without them. "Gloria Jean it's been a lot of years since it happened, can we finally talk about it?"

"I'm not sure I can explain it any better now, but my instincts were strongly in favor of what I did, and I have never felt any regret with my decision."

Trixie was going to raise a reason for Gloria Jean as to why she should have gone through with it but felt she was intruding into private secrets, saying instead, "I'm going in to change. I want to look my best, Lomax always was so handsome." In her bedroom Trixie took out some pictures of their high school days, they all looked so different. She also looked at several pictures she had received from Lomax when he toured Europe with his parents his last year in college. She reviewed one of him in Germany leaning against a fountain, one in France sitting in a sidewalk café, one in Luxembourg in front of a store. At one time Lomax was considerate to both Trixie and Gloria as they were only three years apart in age. Before Trixie married William she had been sweet on Lomax. Trixie remembered like it was yesterday when the family was at dinner on a Sunday in late June when Gloria Jean looked distressed with a furrowed brow, put her fork down not tasting her chocolate Mousse. "I will not marry him, I can't go through with it."

What shocked everyone, they seemed perfectly suited to each other, a perfect couple if there ever was one. Gloria Jean was a pretty, girl, college educated, Lomax was a dashing Navy Ensign, Trixie had been the one to invite Lomax to the house to play tennis. As soon as he saw Gloria Jean, Lomax was a mesmerized young man. As expected Lomax went on enjoying a successful career, inheriting his family's considerable fortune. The consensus of all was

Gloria Jean committed a grievous error in rejecting Commander Lomax Reeding. Nobody knew back then the reason she did, nobody found out since, and nobody knew now. Gloria Jean went into teaching math, was now head of math at her high school, at peace herself, felt no loss when thinking of Lomax Reeding, felt no loss with her life without a husband, in fact felt quite composed, normal and resigned to her chosen style of life. She reminisced how even though the families had made plans, sent out invitations, as soon as the Lomax family returned from Europe the ring went back.

Trixie finished dressing, thought pensively how Gloria Jean was striving to look calm, but was thinking she surely must be tense and excited. Her husband William walked in to their bedroom, announced a shower and a change. "William, you must wear a suit out of respect for Commander Lomax, after all he has commanded ships." William didn't say anything, he just grimaced when Trixie wasn't looking. Trixie continued with her earlier train of thought. "If Gloria Jean would only marry him now it would be a fairytale ending to a poetic love story," she told her thoughts to her husband as he was dressing.

He looked incredulously at his wife. "I suppose you've picked out either Acapulco or the Bahamas for the honeymoon."

Trixie was in the kitchen when William went out to greet Lomax. Gloria Jean was sipping ice tea and perusing pages of advanced algebra under the shading oak trees. Trixie came out with Lomax, her husband Bill, "Why hello Trixie, how well you look."

"Oh," she answered in a calm voice, "you're too kind, thank you. Gloria Jean, you haven't changed a bit."

"Well, Lomax how are you?"

It seemed to Trixie that Gloria Jean's tone of voice was livelier, emotional and richer than it ever sounded since he had arrived. Breaking the mood, Trixie said, "Commander, what can I get you to drink?"

"Double whiskey if I may, thank you."

Trixie looked at the look on Gloria Jean's face reading into it fascination with the presence of Lomax feeling elated everything seemed to be smoothing out like she envisioned.

After an hour of listening to Commander Lomax relate tales of his exploits, relationships with the current four star admiral, his conversations with the Secretary of State, and how he told the Prime Minister when moored for a month at Scapa Flow Naval Base in England about some of our plans for another super carrier. All the stories were centered around Lomax as the central character and all participants in his related tales deferred to him for concluding judgments. His description of his activities was truly spectacular with him as the central figure. After two hours of listening to one anecdote after another involving a celebrity and he the center of all interest everyone began assuming a look of suspicion, their repeated efforts to inject a question or a comment to effect a conversation failed or was rudely repulsed. The commander rambled on, and the relentless monotonous monologue droned on and on. Finally he stood up. "This has been a most joyous occasion for me," he said looking only at Gloria Jean. When he shook hands goodbye with Gloria Jean he gave her a little lingering extra pressure, but Gloria dismissed it as inconsequential. As the Naval staff car drove off, turning at the corner Trixie Catrell simply kept staring for a moment.

William Catrell said, "You used to like that guy?"

Trixie said, "I can't believe the change, he used to be so quiet and modest."

William Catrell said, "That guy is a narcissistic egomaniac so wrapped up in himself he doesn't know anyone else is alive. Why in almost two hours he gave a monologue and frankly I got the distinct feeling there was a little mythology blended in with some of the things he said." No one present disagreed.

Trixie turned to Gloria Jean, grasped her by the arm, "Surely now after what we have seen you can tell us the reason for what you did?"

Gloria Jean saw no reason now not to state her reason, knowing after the display by Lomax no one would question her decision. She began, "When Lomax was in Europe with his mother and father he was taken to all the scenic places but the only pictures he sent to me were of himself only, not any of his mother, his father, none of them together, no pictures of scenery, only of himself which frightened me away."

No one could gauge the impact of Gloria Jean confirming the accuracy of her alarm at marrying a man with egomaniacal tendencies. Everyone who thought Gloria Jean was pining for not having accepted Lomax realized when two years later she married Principal Rolland Harris whom she had been seeing for five years.

The Substitute

Malcom & Taylor collected much of the commercial coin to be had in the style conscious town of Central City, population 40,000. In fact, several customers also came from surrounding small towns just because Malcom & Taylor always sported the latest finery pictured in Elle and Vogue. It was a tradition, and the lofty earned reputation was due to the discriminating buying skills of senior partner Ebanwald Malcolm who journeyed to New York each spring for the last twenty-five years to provide his heavy pursed stylish conscious female clientele the Parisian flavored fashions their gourmand appetites for the latest demanded.

  This year Ebanwald Malcom found the same stairs he had climbed for years suddenly required more effort, more energy to scale and left him uncomfortable and breathless when completing the climb. The three block stroll from the department store to "Bessemer's Café," now felt like six blocks. Thankful to be able to sit as soon as he arrived at the café, as he now would be sweaty, glad to relax, and needing longer now than his usual regimen of a 40 minute lunch hour to feel capable of returning to the store. Ebanwald Malcolm sensed he would be wise to forgo his annual spring buying mission to New York, forget the plays, the refreshing reunions with the wholesalers he knew, dealt with and enjoyed as friends. His annual chess series with Peachy Weinstein would be sorely missed. They were so evenly matched that each game was a speculation who would prevail. He sensed it was time to pass the torch. When he thought about the last few years he grudgingly admitted each of the last several years had become increasingly exhausting. He didn't fly, even if he did the trip would be too much. He always quoted the adage to others, "It's a wise man that knows his limitations." Now, ironically he thought, it applies to me.

At their customary morning meeting in their conference room where they were having coffee, a tradition they followed almost daily since they started in partnership forty years ago in a small store front carpeting business. Bradley Taylor did the carpet laying, floor staining, refinishing, sanding, laying hardwood floors, while Ebanwald Malcom opened the store, took orders, sold carpeting, did the buying, their partnership was so harmonious, they gradually added allied lines, until they owned six stores on the block. Feeling the need for efficiency and recognizing the profits to be achieved in economy of scale they purchased the remaining three stores on the block, razed the block, built a ten story department store and built it and their allied businesses of carpeting and flooring into a cash cow. Ebanwald Malcom specialized in the retail department store while Bradley Taylor shepherded the carpeting and flooring division. They both flourished with great success.

"Brad, I can't make the trip anymore, I'm just getting too old to handle it anymore."

"Eban, you built this store into the finest fashion minded store in the Eastern part of the state. What do you propose to do?"

"Well, you know, all along your son Kenny has worked with me running the store as my assistant with the idea he would step in eventually. Why not ease him into it now? He's made the trip with me twice before over the years, and I think he can deal effectively with the wholesalers. They know I'll be behind Kenny and in touch with him constantly while he's there so it should be alright." It was agreed by all that Kendall Taylor would go to New York and do the buying for Malcom & Taylor.

The following week a man in a dark blue Bradstreet tailored suit with a dark tie, wing tip shoes, a grey narrow brimmed felt hat, and a Kent-Eagle raincoat over his arm entered the wholesale establishment of Weinstein & Associates. There were no associates. When Peachy Weinstein went into business forty-five years ago he added Associates to his business title to give the impression that he was a sizable company. Old peachy had the mind of a calculator, the perspicacity of a seer, the thoroughness of a sheep sheerer, but these gifts were used with restraint and fair play benefiting both himself and the buyer making the business relationship pleasant and profitable to both.

"So my old chess opponent has surrendered to father age eh? So I welcome Mr.

Taylor instead." He rolled his bulk toward Kendall like a charging grizzly, pumped his hand effusively. He smiled, "I know Malcom & Taylor will buy at least $40,000 in men's suits and could with accessories double that, $40,000 in women's Parisian and domestic dresses just as I know the core of the earth is 7,500 degrees Fahrenheit, equal to the surface temperature of outer burning gases on the surface of the sun."

Kenny was both impressed and amused, "What is this Peachy, Science 101?"

Peachy laughed, "Let's leave all the business details for tomorrow. Come, I will treat you to a Turkish cigar that will drive the taste of all others from your mouth and send you a few boxes as my gift to you when you confirm my opinion. Oh Georgia, you will have to escort Mr. Taylor tonight to Ciro's for dinner and the play at Rockefeller Center. He is now the buyer for a customer of over twenty years, we must treat him well."

Georgia was accustomed to these assignments. "Ok, I'll show him around," she said, stepping up and adjusting the knot in Kendall's tie. She put her arm through Kendall's.

She chirped, "Were off Mr. Taylor," and whisked him through the door.

The next morning, Kendall with his briefcase under his arm, came ready to do some buying. Peachy Weinstein himself waited on his best customers being the only one who gave discounts if it was necessary to close the deal. "Well Kenny, what do you think of New York?"

"Not much, too noisy, people are too remote, too commercial, too distant, I can skip it. I wouldn't care to live here if that's what you're asking."

"Well, we're lit up special though aren't we?"

"Yes, if that's what you're after. I like your array of ethnic restaurants though, the selection is extraordinary, I wish I had time to try them all. It's not that I'm a gourmet or anything, I just have a curiosity. I once heard that there are dishes in many cultures that are very similar, they just call them by different names. I found that out to be true about stews."

"Stay a few weeks and find out."

Kenny Taylor was not a frivolous man given to indolent wasting of time and self indulgence, while he was curious enough to find out about the similarities in food in different cultures he regarded devoting time exclusive to it as imprudent. "No, I'll just try one here and there when the opportunity comes up."

Peachy Weinstein took Kendall upstairs to the showing of men's suits, accessories, placed an order for twenty thousand dollars without hesitation. Peachy Weinstein was amazed, even Ebanwald Malcom never moved that fast. What Peachy didn't know was Ebanwald Malcom had spoken with all the other wholesale houses and had given Kenny license to act.

With the men's furnishing business out of the way, Peachy Weinstein turned to the clerk seated at the desk near the door, "Ask Miss Casten to come in here," he said to the clerk sitting at desk. She thumbed the intercom button relaying the request for Miss Casten to appear.

Kendall Taylor was 34 years old, graduated from Indiana University business school, attended the prestigious Wharton School of Business, started in accounts receivable at Malcom & Taylor, then accounts payable, then to budgeting, then assumed the position of Chief Financial Officer and now added head of buying to his resume. Kenny was medium height, 185 pounds, ruggedly handsome, possessed an egalitarian attitude, treated everyone with polite deference making him agreeable and popular with everyone. Most wealthy people were not like that.

Miss Casten glided in with her graceful rhythmic stride. She was the top model at Weinstein's, formerly the top model at Lafontee's & Renes's. Her measurements 38-25-43 exceeded the norms, she was described in the blond rating scale as, "golden," possessed the skill, talent, looks to make any garment desirable to a male buyer. The buyer from Malcom & Taylor was catapulted into a transfixed state of captivity rendered by the wand of the phenomenon called, "love at first sight." Kenny stared motionless as the sphinx in a helpless state of suspension. Miss Casten was accustomed to these reactions but the concentrated intensity of Kenny's stare was of a new realm causing her to redden a bit from this unabashed homage to her beauty. Peachy said, "Miss Casten, you may begin the cavalcade."

Miss Casten rotated in and out of the dressing room wearing one dazzling creation after another driving an additional nail each time sealing the door to Kenny's temple of love. Miss Casten was experienced, she was efficiently performing with perfunctory skill, poised, comfortable with self assurance before the mesmerized, stricken Kenny Taylor who was silent throughout the entire presentation. Miss Casten had impressed buyers before so her attitude was the usual weary, boring feeling with contempt for the ogling buyer who had the usual hint of wishing to buy more than fashions.

When the presentations concluded Peachy noticed Kendall didn't seem inclined to purchase anything, unaware Kenny's mind was filled with visions of Miss Casten sitting across from the kitchen table from him in their mansion in the exclusive subdivision of Bloomingdale adjacent to Central City, Illinois. "Mr. Kendall, er ah Kenny, you're an astute young man. Please take your time and compare prices, you'll see no one will meet my prices. I know you're bored with New York, don't care for it here and you're not having a good time. You need some female companionship to make your stay here pleasant and agreeable. Now Miss Casten would be delighted to show you the town."

Hearing that perked up Kenny's interest. "Well, I'm a stranger to her, would she consider it?" He dared to think she might.

Peachy smiled, he lied, "Would she ever! The girls love a night out, a fine dinner, entertainment, it's an opportunity for them." He had the clerk at the desk summon Miss Casten by intercom again. Peachy said, "I'll introduce you Kenny, she will be eager to go," he lied again. Miss Casten dressed in a plain black skirt, a plain white blouse glided in with her smooth eurhythmic graceful swing adding to Kenny's already total destruction. "Mr. Taylor would like your company this evening at dinner Miss Casten."

"That'll be ok," she said with a quick boring roll of her eyes. "Thank you for the invitation. 1789 Westchester Avenue. What time?"

"How about six thirty?"

"That's ok, but I live with my mother and sister so I won't ask you in because she does not like visitors at night. Call me on your cell phone when you get here and I will come right down."

At seven fifteen they were in an Italian restaurant on Fifth and Broadway, all the bright lights the equal of Las Vegas. She was dressed in a plain modest dress that buttoned at the throat. Kenny didn't know her presence here was all part of her day's work. Kenny in consultation with Miss Casten and the Neapolitan waiter ordered a fine Italian dinner with a vintage Chianti with a reputation of a special smooth sweet taste. Kenny poured the wine for each of them, handed Miss Casten her glass. "Here's to Weinstein & Associates," Kenny said.

"Didn't know you thought that much of us," she laughed.

"I don't, but I do of you."

Oh, oh, here it comes thought Miss Casten. I thought this guy was different. Miss Casten assumed a bored, defensive contemptuous look, feeling she knew what was next, from past experiences it could be a candid crude carnal proposition, that failing, a pricey gift with understanding what the trade off was, I really am smitten with you and want to know you better, join me in Vegas for a week but they all added up to wanting me for a night she bitterly thought, but none persisted and none had rung true. Miss Casten couldn't suppress her undisciplined independence. "Ok, let's cut the wind right here Mr. Taylor. I am not on the ordering list, I'm here or I would lose my job and if you are displeased to hear that just take me home and I'll still thank you for the horderves and wine."

"No, no, Miss... what is your first name?"

"Lillian."

"Lillian, you have me all wrong. Many times a year these past years I think about someone that I have never seen, never heard, never could imagine but when I saw you yesterday I knew it was you all along and now you're here. My business in New York is finished I'll be heading home tomorrow. First I must purchase a limousine so there's enough room for your personal things, because you're coming with me."

Miss Casten looked incredulously at Kenny and his startling comment. "Say, put a stopper in it, all I'm supposed to do is join you for dinner and try to amuse you a little, but I'm not in one the dresses you bought."

"Are you telling me you go out with a lot of the buyers?"

"Yes."

"And they say the same things that I am saying to you now."

"Pretty much, yes."

"Well it's not the same, I mean it. I intend to take you back to Central City tomorrow with me so be ready around noon."

Lillian displayed a sad, weary, disgusted look. "Kenny, just shut up please. If you only knew how often I have heard that kind of talk. I really thought for a while you were a little different than most of the others but you're not, you're just like the rest. Now excuse me while I use the washroom, when I come out you will take me home or I will take a cab, I've lost my appetite."

Kenny watched Lillian's eurhythmic stroll to the bathroom. As soon as she went through the washroom door he took out a square black velvet case and a small envelope and slid them into the bottom of her purse. Kenny took her to the door of her apartment. From the faint light from the hall he could see a small tear in the corner of each of her lovely blue eyes. "What's the matter?" Kenny said.

"Well it's because, well I thought at first you were different, but well, never mind."

"Lillian, I will pick you up at your apartment at noon, I must pick up the limousine I ordered this morning first."

Miss Casten deplored being provided as an escort to buyers by Mr. Weinstein but it was do it or else. She understood it was part of the job, but it didn't mean she had to like it, and didn't. She had to listen to all these wild promises.

Kenny with an overpowering urge got his arm partly around her waist and he received a stinging sharp slap in the face. She wheeled around to go in and Kenny shouted, "Just be ready tomorrow Lillian. I will be by for you."

Lillian Casten shut the door, leaned her back against it and softly wept, the trouble was she liked this guy. Her tears flowed, heavy with regret. She fumbled in her purse for her handkerchief, her fingers fell on an unfamiliar object, she slowly removed a velvet case, she looked at the small envelope with the note, it read:

My Darling Lillian,

I told you I knew my search was over the instant I saw you. I know I am not convincing or eloquent or I could have convinced you. I will pick you up at noon tomorrow in the limousine. I can't wait.

Kenny

Lillian opened the velvet case. It contained a two and a half carat diamond engagement ring and lo and behold a one carat sprinkled diamond wedding ring. It was now eleven o'clock.

Her sister Gwen heard the thumps and slams of things being packed. She poked her half closed sleepy eyes into the dining room, "Why are you packing all that stuff up? For gosh sakes, it's almost midnight Lillian."

"Cause I'm leaving for Central City tomorrow at noon."